ALSO BY

ANNA GAVALDA

I Wish Someone Were Waiting for Me Somewhere
Someone I Loved
Hunting and Gathering
French Leave

BILLIE

Anna Gavalda

BILLIE

*Translated from the French
by Jennifer Rappaport*

Europa
editions

FICTION
GAU

Europa Editions
214 West 29th Street
New York, N.Y. 10001
www.europaeditions.com
info@europaeditions.com

Library of Congress Cataloging in Publication Data is available
ISBN 978-1-60945-249-0

Gavalda, Anna
Billie

Book design by Emanuele Ragnisco
www.mekkanografici.com

Cover photo © BLOOM Image/Getty

Prepress by Grafica Punto Print – Rome

Printed in the USA

CONTENTS

BILLIE

We looked at each other spitefully. He, because he must have thought it was all my fault, and I, because that was no reason to look at me in such a way. Stupid things. I've totally done them so many times since we've known each other, and he has totally enjoyed it and had such a laugh thanks to me—it was wrong of him to blame me just because this time it was going to end badly.

Shit, how could I have known?

I was crying.

"What's up now? Feeling guilty?" he muttered, closing his eyes. "No, how stupid of me . . . guilt, you . . . "

He was too exhausted to get completely mad at me. He didn't have the energy. Plus it was pointless. On that score, we would always agree: Guilt . . . I don't even know how to spell the word.

We were at the bottom of a crevice, or of something geologically very uncomfortable. A type of . . . of rockslide in the Cévennes National Park, where there was no cell phone signal, where there wasn't a sheep's rear end—let alone that of a shepherd—and where no one would ever find us. I had really bashed up my arm, but I could still move it, while he, it was clear, was in a thousand pieces.

I had always known he was brave, but there, really, he was giving me a lesson.

Another one.

He was lying on his back. At first, I had tried to make him a pillow with my sneakers, but as he practically passed out when I raised his head, I lowered it immediately and stopped touching him. It was actually the only moment when he freaked out—he thought he'd really messed up his spinal cord, and was so totally terrified of the idea of ending up paralyzed that he drove me crazy for hours trying to get me either to abandon him in that hole or to finish him off.

Fine. As I had nothing handy with which to properly do him in, we played doctor.

We hadn't met when we were still young enough to play that game, alas, but we would certainly have gotten to it if we had. That thought amused him, which was good because, whether it was hell here or on the other side, that was all I wanted to take with me: a few small abortive smiles, snatched, like that one there.

The rest, frankly, I could leave it.

I pinched him all over, harder and harder. When he suffered, I was thrilled. It was proof his brain was functioning and I wouldn't have to roll him to Saint-Pierre. If not, no problem, I was okay with smashing his skull. I loved him enough.

"Good, seems like everything's working. All you do is squeal so everything's okay, right? In my opinion, in addition to your leg, you've broken your hip or your pelvis. Well, something in this area . . . "

"Hm."

He didn't seem convinced. I felt something was bothering him. I felt I wasn't one hundred percent believable without a white coat and that thingamoscope around my neck. He looked at the sky, frowning and chewing his cheek like an old grump.

I knew that expression of his, I knew them all, in fact, and I understood that doubt was still pricking him.

Yeah, that was the right word.

"Naaaaaah, Francky, naaaah . . . I'm hallucinating, I don't believe it. You don't really want me to jerk you off to check it too?"

" . . . "

"Really?"

I could see he was struggling with all his might to give his best dying face, but as for me, I had no issues of decency. More of efficiency. The situation was serious and I really couldn't take the risk of bumping him off just because I wasn't his type.

"Uh . . . it's not that I don't want to, you know? But really, you . . . "

It made me think of Jack Lemmon in the last scene of *Some Like It Hot*. Like him, I began to run out of arguments so I had to pull out the only thing I had left to stop him from busting my balls:

"I'm a girl, Franck."

And then, you see . . . then, if I were in the middle of giving a very serious presentation on Friendship, the cross-disciplinary type with diagrams, slides, mini bottles of water and all the rest, to explain where it came from, out of what material it was made, and how to look out for fakes, well, I would say, "Please, freeze the frame," and with my mouse, I would point to his reply:

Those three little rotten and cheerful words muttered with a super bad imitation of a smile by a human being who didn't even know if he was going to live or die, or continue to suffer but without ever fucking again:

"*Well, nobody's perfect.*"

Yes, for once, I was sure of myself and too bad for those who haven't seen it, who understand nothing about the film, and who will never know how to recognize the virtuous friend in a poor transvestite. I can't help them.

So, because it was him, because it was me, and because we had still managed to stick together and support each other in such a hopeless moment, I climbed over him in order to rest my good arm on his lower belly.

I just grazed it.

"Good," he grumbled after a moment. "I'm not asking you to go all out, girl. Just touch it and we won't talk about it anymore."

"I don't dare."

He let out a deep sigh.

I understood his chagrin. We had both been through situations that were so much more embarrassing than this where I had hardly been at my best, and I had rocked him to sleep with so many really crude and abominable stories about my promiscuous sex life that I was hardly credible.

Honestly, not at all, not at all, not at all!

But I was serious . . . I didn't dare.

We can never know in advance what's going to happen when we nuzzle up to the sacred. My hand still steady, I suddenly realized there was a world of difference between my sexual escapades and his cock. I could have touched them all if necessary, but not his, no, not his; this time it was me who was giving the lesson all alone for once.

I always knew I adored him, but I had never had the occasion to measure how much I respected him, and now, the answer, I was holding it: a few millimeters.

Let it be the infinite measure of my modesty. Of our modesty.

Of course, I already knew I wasn't going to let myself be hindered for very long by this pussycat of a problem but in the meantime, I was the first to be surprised. Seriously, I was shocked to see myself so squeamish. Intimidated, timid, almost a virgin again! It was like Christmas.

Okay, let's go. Enough bullshit. Let's get to work, virgin!

To relax him, I began by tapping around his belly button while humming a nursery rhyme: "Peck lil' hen, peck all day. Raise your tail, then go away!" but it didn't help much. Then I laid down beside him, closed my eyes, and rested my lips on his . . . uh . . . auditory canal. I concentrated and whispered very quietly, no, even quieter than that, while blowing saliva bubbles into his ear with all the necessary annoying little coos, what I guessed were the worst or the best of his most locked-away fantasies, all while tracing with a lazy, distracted fingernail the U that formed the seams of his fly.

The hairs of his ears retracted in terror and my honor was saved.

He cursed. He smiled. He laughed. He said you're a pest. He said give it a rest. He said you're a jerk. He said it's gonna work. He said, but you're going to stop, right? He said I hate you and he said I adore you.

But all that was a long time ago. When he still had the energy to finish his sentences and I had no idea I would cry in front of him one day. Now, night was falling, I was cold, I was hungry, I was dying of thirst and I was going crazy because I didn't want him to suffer. And if I were a little bit honest, I would finish those sentences for him, adding "because of me" at the end.

But I'm not honest.

I was sitting next to him, my back against a rock, and I was slowly wilting.

I was shedding guilty feeling after guilty feeling.

With an effort I could never have imagined, he peeled his arm from his body and his hand came to touch my knee. I rested mine on it and this made me even weaker.

I didn't like him taking advantage of my better nature, the little vulture. It was disloyal.

After some time, I asked him:
"What's that sound?"
". . ."
"Do you think it's a wolf? Do you think there are wolves?"
And as he didn't answer, I yelled:
"Answer me, for God's sake! Say something! Tell me yes, tell me no, tell me to fuck off, but don't leave me here alone. Not now . . . I'm begging you."

It wasn't him I was speaking to. It was to myself. To my stupidity. To my shame. To my lack of imagination. He would never have abandoned me, and if he didn't speak, it was only because he had lost consciousness.

For the first time in a long time, he no longer had that reproachful look and the idea that he must be in less pain gave me courage: one way or another we were going to get out of this mess. It was inevitable. We hadn't come all this way to play out a mini version of *Into the Wild* in a hole in the Lozère.

Fuck no, that would be too embarrassing.

I was reconsidering the situation. First of all, those weren't wolves, but bird cries. Owls or something. Plus, you couldn't die from a few broken bones. He didn't have a fever, he wasn't losing blood, he was complaining of pain, okay, but he wasn't in danger. The best thing to do for the moment was to sleep in order to get my strength back and tomorrow, at dawn, when I would be fed up once again with this shitty countryside, I would leave.

I would go through that filth of a forest, I would go through that muck of a mountain, and I would drop a fucking helicopter into that valley.

That's it. End of discussion. I would solemnly swear to move my derrière, and it would careen across the plateau. Because hiking with that family earlier, *Left! Right! Left! Right!*, with stupid, loaded donkeys and pack burros who were completely stressed out, that was fun for, like, two minutes.

Sorry, guys, but for us, all this hiking crap sucks!

Do you hear me, babe? Did you hear what I just said? Bet your life on it, as long as I'm alive, you won't take your last breath in the boonies. Never. I'd rather die.

I stretched out again, grumbled, then got up to clean off my sleeping area and toss the pile of rocks that were digging into my back before wedging myself up against him again like a recumbent statue.

But I couldn't fall sleep.

The little goblins living in my brain had dropped too much acid.

Up there, a Breton pipe-band was being remixed to a techno beat.

Hell.

I was concentrating so hard I could no longer hear myself think and no matter how much I clung to him and squeezed him with my arms, I was still cold.

I was freezing, DJ Grumpy was destroying the three courage neurons I had left, so a few tears more nimble than the others managed to slip out.

Ah, fuck, I had really lost it.

To force them back, I tipped my head toward the sky and . . . ah then . . . Ooohh . . .

It wasn't so much the stars that had made me speechless, we had already seen gobs of them on our trek, it was their chore-ography. *Pling!* They lit up *Gling!* one after the other in rhythm. I didn't even know *Ding!* that it was possible.

They shone so brightly it was almost tacky.

As though they were LEDs or brand-new toys barely out of the box. As if someone had turned up the dimmer switch.

It was . . . magnificent . . .

Suddenly, I wasn't alone, and I turned to Franck to wipe my face on his shoulder.

Ah, yes, have some decency, you deadbeat. You have to stop snuffling when God lends you his disco ball.

Are there spring tides for galaxies as for oceans or was this display just for me? A big up to me from the Milky Way? A tremendous rave party of Tinkerbells come to sprinkle a bundle of gold dust on my head to help me recharge my batteries?

They came from everywhere and it seemed like they were making the night warmer. I felt as though I were getting a tan in the dark. I felt the world had turned upside down. That I was no longer at the bottom of the abyss whining about my misery, but on stage . . .

Yes, no matter how low I went (how low I got?) (well, in short, even if I made myself flat as a crêpe), I was on top.

I was in a huge open-air concert hall, like the Zénith in Paris, the type that went from one end of the Earth to the other, right in the middle of a killer song, and with all those lighters, and those screens, and all those thousands of magic candles that the angels turned toward me, I had to show I was worthy. I was no longer entitled to cry about my plight, and I wished Francky could have enjoyed it too.

He wouldn't have been able to tell the difference between the Big Dipper and the Little Dipper either, but he would have been so happy to see so much beauty, so happy. Because that was him, the artist of the two of us. It was thanks to his sensitivity that we had succeeded in getting out of our shithole and it was because of him that the universe had taken out its sparkly tuxedo.

To thank him.

To pay him respect.

To tell him: "You, little one, we know you. Yes, indeed, we

know you . . . For a long time, we've been watching you and have noticed that you're obsessed with beauty. All your life, you've done nothing but look for it, care for it, and invent it. And uh, well . . . look . . . for the effort you've made . . . Look at yourself in this mirror in the sky . . . This evening, we're paying you back with interest. Your friend, she's quite vulgar, she does nothing but spit all over the place and swear like an old slut. I wonder who let her in. While you . . . you're family . . . Come, son . . . Come dance with us."

I was speaking out loud.

In all modesty and for a boy who couldn't hear me, I had just spoken on behalf of the universe!

It was stupid, but it was cute . . .

It showed how much I loved him.

Uh . . . otherwise . . . one last thing, Mr. Universe . . . (and right when I said that, I saw James Brown), no, two things, in fact.

First, you leave my friend there where he is. It's not worth the trouble to call him, he won't come. Even if I embarrass him, he'll never leave me here. That's how it is and even you can't do anything about it.

 Second, I apologize for the way I'm speaking.

It's true, I overdo it, but every time I offend your ears, it's not because I lack respect, it's because of the frustration at not finding the right words quickly enough. It's a man's world, you know.

I feel good, he answered.

* * *

I was looking at all the stars, searching for ours.

Because we had one, for sure. Not one each, unfortunately,

but one for the two of us. A little nightlight to share. Yes, a little lamp we'd found the day we met and who, in good years and bad, had done good work up to that point.

Sure, she'd screwed up a bit a few hours back, but everything had blown over since then . . .

She was getting all dolled up, the little doll.

She was using up all her Sephorus glitter spray.

Hey, it was only natural. She was our star! And if her friends were going off to the fireworks, she wasn't going to be left behind.

I was looking for her.

I looked them all over in order to find her because I had stuff to say to her, to remind her about.

I was looking for her to convince her to help us one more time.

Despite us.

Despite me, especially.

Yes. Since I wasn't infalliable...infalloble... Oh, fine, since everything was my fault, it was up to me to keep talking her pointy ears off so she would reactivate the hotline.

The others, they were beautiful too, but I really didn't give a fuck about them—sorry, I mean, I couldn't care less about them—while as for her, if I put all my heart and soul into describing the situation, I was sure she would soften up again.

I think I found her.

I think it was that one there, all the way up in the air, hovering above my fingertip, say, and billions of years away.

So little, so cute, like a teensy Swarovski crystal, and slightly misaligned in the sky.

Slightly set back from the herd . . .

Yes, she was the one. XXS, solitary and wary, but giving it all she had. The one who was twinkling with all her might. Who was too happy to be there. Who loved to sing and who knew all the lyrics by heart.

Who was sparkling beautifully in the night.

Who would be the first to bed and the first to wake up. Who was going to be out every night. Who had been partying for trillions of years and who always had that much flair.

Hey, was I wrong?

Hey, was it you?

Oh, excuse my bad manners. Was it you, *Mademoiselle?*

Hey . . . can I talk to you for a minute?

Can I tell you again who we are, Franck and me, so you will love us this time for eternity?

I took her silence for a sigh of resignation, as in, hey, you're wearing me out, you losers; but fine . . . you're lucky, it's a slow dance and I don't have a date. So go ahead, I'm listening. Sell me on your story quickly so I can go back to munching my Milky Way.

I sought Franck's hand, squeezed it with all my might, and took a minute to get us in order.

Yes, I got us all spruced up, all polished and combed, in order to show you our best side, and after that I launched into our story.

Like Buzz Lightyear.
To infinity and beyond . . .

His name is Franck because his mother and grandmother adored the singer Frank Alamo (*Biche, oh ma biche, Da doo ron ron, Allô Maillot 38-37*, and all that. Yes, there really are songs with those titles) and my name is Billie because my mother was crazy about Michael Jackson (*Billie Jean is not my lover / She's just a girl*, et cetera).

In other words, we didn't start out in life with the same namesake and we weren't necessarily destined to hang out together one day.

His mom and his grandma took such great care of him when he was little that to show his appreciation he bought them a Return of the Yéyés CD, tickets to Frank Alamo's Yéyé revival concert as well as to a musical, a Blu-ray DVD, and even the cruise that went with all that.

And when Dadooron Frank kicked the bucket, Franck asked for a day off, went looking for them on the train to the funeral, moved them up to first class, and accompanied them to the front of I don't remember what church.

All that so he could support them in their grief as they hummed Alamo's *Sur un dernier signe de la main* while his coffin was being loaded into the hearse . . .

As for my story, I don't know if my mother had other kids after me whom she called Bad or Thriller nor if she cried when Bambi disappeared into the void since she took off when I was a year old. (I have to admit I was quite a pain in the ass . . .)

(That's what my father told me one day: "Your mother took off because you were too much of a pain in the ass. It's true, you did nothing but bawl all the time . . . ") (Hey, I don't know how many shrinks it would take to get over such an explanation, but loads of them, if you want my opinion!)

Yes, one morning, she left and we never heard from her again.

My stepmother never liked my first name. She said it sounded like a guy's name—a guy with a bad reputation—I never had the guts to contradict her. Anyway, don't count on me to badmouth her. It's true she's a bitch but it's not really her fault. Plus this evening, I'm not here to talk about her. We all have our shit to deal with.

So, voilà, little star, that's it for childhood.

Franck rarely speaks about his and when he does, it's only to distance himself from it. And as for me, I didn't have a childhood.

The fact that I still like my first name, given the circumstances, is quite an achievement, I think.

Only the brilliant Michael Jackson could perform such a feat . . .

* * *

Franck and I went to the same junior high. But it wasn't until our last year there, the only year we were in the same class, that we spoke to each other. Since then we've admitted that we noticed each other the morning of the first day of our first year. Yes, we picked each other out immediately, but unconsciously we avoided each other all those years because both of us sensed that the other was in such a sorry state and we didn't want to suffer even one ounce more than we were already.

It's true, too, that I specifically sought out the company of girls who dressed like Polly Pocket. All cutesy with long hair, their own bedrooms, packs of fancy cookies, and a mom who happily signed the correspondence that came home from school. I did everything I could so they would like me and invite me home with them as often as possible.

Alas, there were times when I was a bit less popular . . . in the winter especially . . . I didn't really understand it until much later, but it was a matter of . . . of a hot-water tank . . . and also of . . . uh . . . odor . . . of . . . fuck . . . but hey, I'm thinking about it so much that I'm starting to get embarrassed again. Okay, let's move on.

All this time, I lied so much about my story that I had to write down the main points in order not to mix up one school year with another.

At my place, I behaved like a hungry animal who smelled bacon next door but couldn't have any since no one was bringing it home, but at school, I was always calm. At any rate, I wouldn't have had the necessary energy to be on the defensive twenty-four hours a day. You have to have experienced it to understand, but those who have, they know exactly what I'm talking about: on the defensive . . . always, always . . . And especially when things were calm. Calm moments, they were the worst, they . . . no, never mind . . . nobody gives a damn.

One day, in my social studies class, the teacher, Monsieur Dumont, without realizing it, taught me something about my life. The underclass, he said. The teacher said it just like that, like exportation of wealth or the silting of Mont Saint Michel, but I remember, my face turned bright red with embarrassment. I didn't know there was a word in the dictionary invented specifically to indicate where I came from. Because I was well placed to know it, this milieu; it's not necessarily apparent to the naked eye. The proof is in the fact that social workers have never shown up . . . If you don't stick out and you go to school every day, that safe haven of childhood, you get by easily, and my stepmother, I won't say that she looked bourgeois, but really, people would treat her with respect when she went to the supermarket, they said hello, how are the kids? And so on.

I never knew where she bought the oil for the furnace.

The oil was there, maybe it was little mice or Santa's reindeer, but for me, the great mystery of my childhood would remain those fucking empty bottles of oil. *Where* did they come from? Where?

The great, great mystery . . .

* * *

It wasn't public school that got me out of there. It wasn't the teachers or the sweet Mademoiselle Gisèle who prepared us for communion or the students' parents who were always shocked by the weight of our backpacks or those sophisticated girlfriends of mine who listened to public radio and read books and all that. No, it was him (and I was pointing to him in the darkness). It was Franck Muller.

Yes, him there . . . that weakling Franck Mumu, who was six months younger than me and six inches shorter, who lost his balance every time you tapped him on the shoulder and who was always acting like a pain in the ass at the bus stop. He was the one who saved me.

Him alone.

Honestly, I'm not angry at anyone and even now, you see, I'm telling you all this and it's okay, I'm doing well these days. That was a long time ago. Such a long time ago that it isn't really even me, in fact . . .

Fine, I admit, I always feel a bit anxious when I have to fill out paperwork. Family name, place of birth, and all that. Right away my stomach drops, but it's okay, it passes. It passes quickly.

The only thing is that I never want to see them again. Never, never, never . . . I never want to go back there, never. Not for anyone's marriage, not for anyone's funeral, not for anything. Also, whenever I pass a car with a license plate from my region, I immediately look elsewhere to regain my composure.

At one point—and as I don't think I'll have time to tell you about it in detail tonight I'll just give you a summary—during one period of my life when I kept screwing up, when my childhood came back to haunt me too often, and when I got into the habit of hitting the bottle, as they say, to hide from the world, I listened to Franck and hit the reset button.

I completely wiped out my hard drive in order to restart in safe mode.

It was a long process and I think I succeeded, but all I ask for in return is to never see them again.

Never.

Not even when they're dead, incinerated, not even as a scrap of cloth in a grave.

And even there, you see, I'm going to be honest for once; if you were to say to me: "Okay, I'll send you two stretchers, a ham sandwich, and a case of San Pellegrino, but in exchange, you give a little wave to your stepmother or to any of those jerks," well, I would say no.

No.

I would say no and I would find some other way to get us out of here.

* * *

So, there you have it, we went to the same junior high in a

small town with less than three thousand inhabitants in what they call a rural region. But "rural" is too nice a way to put it. You'd expect to see hills and streams. The area where I'm from doesn't have much of that. It was, is, an area of France that hasn't been irrigated for a long time and is rotting as a result.

Yes, rotting . . . dying . . . A land where folks drink too much, smoke too much, put too much faith in the lottery, and pass down their poverty to their family and pets.

A world in which everyone commits suicide in the same way: by slowly burning out and dragging the weakest down with them.

When you hear about disaffected young people setting cars on fire, it's always in working-class suburbs, but in the countryside, my dear, life is not easy, you know!

For us to burn cars, some would have to pass by!

When you live in the countryside and are not like others, it's even worse.

Of course, there will always be people passing through, whether politicians, association types, organic foodies, or whatever sweet liars who will tell you I'm exaggerating, but I know them, these people . . . Yes, I know them . . . They're like the ones from social services: at the end of the day, they only see what we want to show them . . .

And I understand them.

I understand them because I've become like them, too.

Whenever I'm going to or coming back from the Rungis market, which is at least four times a week, I know exactly where I need to focus on what I'm doing. Yes, there are exactly two places where I completely stick to the road and where I am extremely careful to maintain a safe distance. And do you know why? Because in those spots, between Paris and Orly let's say, there are two little piles of garbage on the roadside, at street level.

Fine, it's true, they're ugly, but the problem is that they aren't really garbage in fact . . . No, they're houses. They're the bedrooms of little girls who are always on the defensive . . .

Okay, let's speed things along. As I said earlier, we all have our shit to deal with. I suffered so much that I became an arrogant monster, and my arrogance is what I can best offer to little Billie from Highway A6.

Look, little girls, look at me in my old delivery van all beat up and filled with flowers. I'm proof that it's possible to have a life someday . . .

S o, yes, we noticed each other but avoided contact all that time because we were like the scourge of Jacques-Prévert Junior High.

Me, because I was from the Morels (no, that's not the name of a town in the sticks or an area with mushrooms, it's . . . I don't know . . . I never knew in fact . . . a junkyard . . . a sort of artisanal realm . . . a type of waste recycling center where nothing is ever sorted . . . everyone says "the Gypsies" but we weren't Gypsies, there was just my stepmother's family, her uncles, half-sisters, my half-brothers and all that . . . people from the Morels in other words) and I walked a mile and a half every morning and every evening to go to a different bus stop, the farthest possible from their mess and from my Home Sweet Mobile Home for fear that the other kids wouldn't let me sit next to them on the bus, and he, because he was too different from everyone else.

Because he didn't love girls, only liked them, because he was good at drawing but bad at sports, because he was slight and allergic to anything and everything, because he always hung out by himself and disappeared completely into his own world and because he waited to be last in line at the cafeteria to avoid the noise and the stampede to get through the turnstiles.

I know, little star, I know, it sounds like a crappy cliché, the way I'm telling it; the sickly little queer and his Cosette from the garbage dump, I admit, it lacks subtlety. But what would you like me to say instead? That I live in a regular house in the winter and add in a moped and two chain bracelets to make it sound less like I come from a lousy soap opera?

Well, no . . . I would like to but I can't . . . Because that's how we are. That's the story of our early lives. Neverland and Da doo ron ron. Rebels without a cause. But I'm going to force myself to pretty things up so that it won't sound so sad . . .

So, Beat It.

Just Beat It.

And so? It's not so bad, right? I'm not going to try to convince you I was groped or anything gross like that.

Luckily, that wasn't the thing at my house.

At our house, things were tough, but no one touched little girls' panties.

Phew, what a relief, right, little star?

And then, you know, I think it wasn't all that cliché. I think that in all the schools in France and elsewhere, whether in the countryside or in the towns, the study halls are full of people, like us.

People who struggle against invisibility, who are disconnected from themselves, who hold their breath from morning till night and who die sometimes, who finally give up one day if no one helps them out or if they don't manage on their own . . . Plus I think I'm telling the story quite delicately, in fact. Not to spare you discomfort or me any criticism, but because the evening of one of my birthdays, my twenty-second, I think, I pressed reset.

I rebooted in front of him and swore that I was done. That I would never hurt myself again.

And little Cosette, maybe she lacks imagination, but she does keep her promise.

We did such a good job avoiding each other, we nearly missed each other for good.

We were in the middle of the academic year. There were still a few months left to get through and then we would have to decide what to do next based on our strengths and weaknesses and what we'd done well at in school. I wanted to get a job as quickly as possible while he . . . I don't know . . . when I looked at him from afar, he made me think of the Little Prince, especially since he had the same yellow scarf. No one could tell what he was going to become.

Yes, there were still several weeks left for us to ignore one another before we would be done with the ghost of the other and all it represented forever.

Except that, lo and behold: we were owed a second act . . .

Was it God who was too embarrassed by what he'd let happen until then and wanted to make amends to sooth his heartburn, or was it you, Mademoi—? Okay, enough with the formalities, was it you? I feel like I'm presenting my case to an officer at the unemployment office. I don't know who did it nor why, but in any case, it was exactly like Charlie and his gold ticket in Willy Wonka's chocolate bar. It was . . . really lucky.

Ah shit, I'm starting to cry again and I'm turning again toward my broken bolster so no one will see.

* * *

We were introduced to Alfred de Musset, and when I said earlier that it wasn't school or the teachers who had gotten me out of the Morels, I wasn't being fair. Because . . . well, given that my teachers didn't like me, it really hurts me to praise them, but there you have it, it's true . . . I owe them more than a few moments of rest during the school year.

Without my French teacher Madame Guillet, and without

her mania for theater and *live performance*, as she called it, I
would surely be some sort of zombie today.

> *Don't Fool with Love*
> *Don't Fool with Love*
> *Don't*
> *Fool*
> *with*
> *Love*

Oh . . . How I love to say it, that title . . .

Our mother hen of a teacher arrived one morning with three little rattan baskets from her kitchen. In the first were folded pieces of paper—the scenes we were to perform; in the second were the names of the girls in the class to decide the role of Camille, and in the last basket, the names of the boys to decide the role of Perdican.

When I heard that fate had chosen Franck Mumu for my performance partner, not only did I not know that the play in question was not about animals (I had understood "Pelican") but also, I remember, I completely lost my composure . . .

The lottery was held on purpose the day before Easter break, so that we would have time to learn our dialogue, but for me it was a disaster. How was I supposed to concentrate on learning the least little thing by heart during the fucking vacation? It was over before it started. I had to refuse. And there was no way he could be my partner because then it would be my fault that he got a bad grade. Vacations for me were synonymous with . . . the opposite of learning anything. Thus all this lace-frilled-shirt bullshit written in small type, it wasn't even worth thinking about.

So when he came up to me at the end of class, I didn't see him because I had already tied myself up in knots.

"If you want, we can go to my grandmother's house to practice . . . "

It was the first time I was hearing his voice and . . . Oh . . . Oh my God . . . that really did me good . . . that loosened me up right away. It stopped me from stressing out.

Why? Because it let me avoid having to *ask* something of a teacher . . .

As he thought I was hesitating (no, actually, it was just, wow, the prospect of spending two weeks there), he added timidly:

"She's a seamstress . . . Maybe she could make us costumes."

I went to this lady's house every day and each time stayed a little longer than the day before. I even slept there one night because the film version of Guy de Maupassant's *The Necklace* was playing on TV and Franck invited me to watch it with him.

As for the Morels, for once, they didn't bother me too much. It's awful to say, but in our world, you get respect if you spend the night with someone early on.

I had a boyfriend, I was dating. At fifteen years old, I was finally screwing, so I wasn't such a loser after all.

Of course, I couldn't help having such totally humiliating and dirty thoughts; first of all, I was used to it, second, as soon as they let me run off, I no longer gave a damn.

My stepmother even paid for me to get new clothes for the occasion. A boyfriend, that was impressive, more so than good grades.

If I had known, I said to myself while looking at my first pair of passably stylish jeans, if I had known, I would have invented tons of "pelicans" before this . . .

Without knowing it and in countless ways that were impossible to analyze at the moment, Franck's simple existence—not even "in my life," no, just his existence—changed the situation.

Mine at least.

It was the only vacation of my childhood and the most beautiful one of my life.

Ah . . . what a pain in the ass . . .
My little bolster.

What really bothered me in the beginning was how calm it was. Since Franck's grandmother left us alone and because he spoke so quietly, I felt as though there were a corpse in the next room. He wouldn't stop asking, "How are you doing? How are you doing?"—because he saw quite clearly that I wasn't doing well at all. I answered fine, fine, but really, I was super uncomfortable.

And then I got used to it . . .

Just like at school, I let my guard down and changed my attitude.

The first time I visited, we went into the dining room where it was so clean that no meal could ever have been served there. It smelled strange . . . like old people . . . sadness . . . We sat facing each other, and he suggested that we begin by re-reading our scene together once through before figuring out how we would rehearse.

I was embarrassed. I didn't understand a thing.

I understood so little that I read the text like an idiot. As if I were deciphering Chinese.

Finally he asked if I had even read the play or at least our section, and when I didn't respond right away, he closed his book and looked at me without saying anything.

I felt my fangs coming out again. I didn't want him to beat me over the head with that bullshit from the fourteenth century. I wanted to learn my required lines like gobbledygook from earlier times, you know, sounding it out but without regard for the meaning, but I didn't want him to act like a teacher with me. I was fed up with people who put me in my place all the time by making me feel like a piece of shit. Already at school, I kept my trap shut to avoid any extra trouble, but not there, not in that room that reeked of Polident. He had to stop looking at me like that or I would leave. I could no longer stand anyone staring at me all the time. I just couldn't.

"I love your first name . . . "

It made me happy even if I thought to myself: well, for sure, it's a boy's name . . . but right away he set me straight:

"It's the name of a marvelous singer . . . Do you know Billie Holiday?"

I shook my head.

No, of course not . . . I didn't know anything.

He told me he would play her music for me someday and asked me to follow him.

"Come, sit on the couch . . . There . . . I'm going to read to you . . . Here, take a cushion . . . Make yourself comfortable . . . Like you're in a movie theater . . . "

Since I'd never been to the movies, I preferred to sit on the floor.

He stationed himself in front of me and began.

First he explained to me all the characters using language I could understand:

"So, here it goes . . . There's an old man called the Baron . . . when the play begins he's all wound up because he's expecting any minute now the return of his son Perdican whom he hasn't seen in years—Perdican had left to study in Paris—and his niece Camille whom he'd raised when she was little and whom he hasn't seen for a long time because he'd sent her to a convent . . . Don't make that face, it was what they did at the time . . . The

convent was like boarding school for the daughters of the aristo-
crats. They learned to sew, to embroider, to sing, to become perfect wives and also that way everyone was sure they remained vir-
gins . . . Camille and Perdican hadn't seen each other for ten
years. They grew up under the same roof and adored each other.
Like brother and sister and surely a bit more if you want my opinion . . . The education of these young people cost a pretty penny,
and what the Baron wanted now was to marry them to each other.
Precisely because they loved each other and also because it would
allow him to recoup his costs. Oh yeah . . . 6,000 écus even . . .
okay? You're still with me? Good, I'll continue then. Perdican
and Camille each had a chaperone . . . Have you seen *Pinocchio*?
So imagine a Jiminy Cricket if you prefer . . . Someone who takes
care of them and keeps an eye on them forever so they stay on
the right path. For Perdican, this was Blazius, his tutor, in other
words, his personal teacher when he was a kid, and for Camille,
this was Dame Pluche. Maître Blazius was a fatso who thought
only about his next drink and Dame Pluche was an old bat who
thought only about fondling her rosary and saying *tsk tsk* to all
the men who came too close to her Camille. Dame Pluche was a
mean, screwed up person, well, frankly, not screwed at all, and
there was no reason to expect Camille to be any different . . . "

Even when he summed it up for me that way, I couldn't get
over it. I even started to have doubts . . . Was this really the
assignment the teacher had given us? Was it really that risqué?
I hadn't gotten that impression . . . For starters, the guy's name,
Alfred de Musset, it made him sound like an old fogey in musty
pince-nez and I . . . Okay, I was smiling, and since I was smiling, Franck Mumu was happy, too. He was exhilarated and
turning cartwheels to keep my attention.
    Without knowing it, he was giving me my first break. The
first performance of my life.

When he had finished presenting the characters to me, he checked that I had everything down by asking me a bunch of very specific little questions:

"Sorry, it's not to trick you . . . It's just to be sure that you'll be able to follow the play later, you understand?"

I said yeah, sure, but I really didn't give a shit about the play. All I understood was that a human being was paying attention to me and speaking to me nicely. It was no longer schoolwork but science fiction.

Then he read me *Don't Fool with Love*. Or rather, he acted it out for me. For each character, he used a different voice and when the chorus was speaking, he climbed on a stool.

For the Baron, he acted like a baron; for Blazius, he acted like a fat little half-drunk grandpa; for Bridaine, a dirty little grandpa who thought about nothing but food; for Dame Pluche, an old bat who spoke through pursed lips; for Rosette, a pretty country girl, but totally naive; for Perdican, a handsome boy who no longer knew if he wanted just to fuck or to get hitched; and for Camille, a girl who wasn't all that hip, but rather straight as an arrow, unimaginative. Well . . . in the beginning . . .

An eighteen-year-old girl who knew nothing about life and who was like one of those candles you light in church: super simple, super pure, and super white, but burning like crazy.

Yes, completely exploding on the inside . . .

I was . . . enthralled.

Exactly like before when I tilted my head to hold back my tears and saw the whole sky.

It was as if I had planted a smile on the cushion I was grasping in my arms.

I did nothing but smile.

At one point, when he was playing Perdican saying to

Camille in a slightly drunk and disdainful tone: "My dear sister, the nuns taught you what they know; but believe me, it's not all you'll know; you won't die without falling in love," he snapped the book shut.

"Why are you stopping?" I asked, worried.

"Because it's the end of our scene and it's time for a snack. Are you coming?"

In the kitchen, while drinking I no longer remember what, some Orangina I think, and while eating his grandma's rubbery madeleines, I couldn't stop myself from thinking out loud:

"It sucks for the teacher to make us stop there . . . I'm dying to know how she answers."

He smiled, "I agree, but the problem is that after this scene, there are massive amounts of texts . . . long, long monologues . . . It would be tough to learn them . . . But it's really a shame because the most beautiful part of this scene, you'll see, comes all the way at the end, when Perdican gets upset and explains to Camille that yes, all men are scoundrels and yes, all women are sluts, but there's nothing more beautiful in the world than what happens between a scoundrel and a slut when they love each other."

I smiled at him.

We didn't say anything else to each other, but at that moment, the two of us already knew what would happen next.

We pretended to finish our drinks as if it were no big deal, but we knew.

We knew, and each knew the other knew too.

We knew it was our last chance and we were getting our revenge for all those years of solitude spent amid the scoundrels and the sluts of the whole world.

Yes, we said nothing and looked out the window to reduce the tension, but we knew.

We knew it was true, that we were beautiful too.

I could spend the whole night telling you what happened next. Those two weeks with him, talking, learning, working, rehearsing, arguing with each other, reconciling, throwing my book, getting irritated, giving up, having a fit, starting over, rehearsing one more time and working again . . .

I could spend the night telling you because for me, my life began then.

And that's not just a figure of speech, little star, it's a quote from a birth certificate, so don't fool with that, please. You'll upset me.

* * *

We had decided to meet each other every afternoon to practice the scenes we had learned that morning and very quickly I realized I needed to find somewhere besides that lovely home of mine in order to get some peace and quiet.

I tested out several places: the back of a wrecked car, the porch of an old sawmill, the washhouse, but it became a game for my stepsister's little rug rats (or let's say the kind of stepsister someone like me would have, the type from the Morels) to follow me nonstop and get on my nerves, and finally, I ended up in the cemetery and sat down in a crypt.

All those crosses, all those bones, all that debris of shattered stones and rusted iron, it calms you down right away, and it was perfect for coaxing out that pain in the ass Camille with her mania for crucifixes.

I hadn't intended to end up there, but really, it turned out well . . .

I don't know if it was the location, if the dead had decided to give me a little help because they were bored and wanted to kill time, but I still can't get over how quickly and easily I learned my lines.

Since I kept the old book with the play safe and sound, I ended up re-reading our scene for fun and, each time, I had to pinch myself to believe it. How did we do it? How did I do it? I, who still don't know the multiplication tables and who was at a loss as soon as a teacher asked us to learn five lines by heart?

I don't know . . . I think it was in order to be worthy of Franck Muller . . . So I wouldn't let him down . . . to thank him for having spoken to me so nicely the first day . . .

That's silly, isn't it?

And then . . . I would be incapable of explaining it properly, but it seemed to me that I had gotten my lousy revenge on a world and on people who, in reality, had ignored me for so long.

I had nothing left to prove to anyone.

Nothing.

I just wanted to make Franck happy and to escape.

I was too young at the time to understand and I don't have words enough to articulate it today, but I had the impression— when I was curled up in my crypt learning the lines of this girl who wouldn't stop nagging and nagging and nagging some more, to get an answer to the crazy questions that were eating at her—that I was taking advantage of it too. Yes, that I was worming my way into her obsessive mind so that I could steal a little bit of her courage and get the hell away by following her example.

What I must have told myself without knowing it is that if I gave the right answers and in so doing allowed Franck Muller to perform his role as well as possible, well, I would no longer be from the Morels.

I would be . . . my own person. Just me. I would be from this abandoned crypt. From my minuscule chapel.

Yes, I was hidden there, sitting in the middle of the rubble, listening to the delirium of this little bourgeois girl who had never suffered and who wanted everything, who wanted to take the whole kitty before even playing a hand, or who preferred not to play, or rather who preferred not to live at all than to live like the others, and all I had to do was hold her close so she could help me reach her outsized desires.

Because even if I didn't agree with her obsessions, I admired her.

I knew she was wrong. I knew that the good nuns had brainwashed her and that it suited her, because she was afraid to go out into the unknown. I knew she would let her pride get the better of her and that she was going to screw up her life because of her lousy, stubborn prudishness about sex. I knew that if she, like me, had just taken a little detour to the Morels she would have calmed down right away and would have imagined her life with more humility, but in the meantime, for that reason precisely, she was the best teammate I could hope for in order to escape.

She was so stubborn and uptight that she would never give up and if I took care of my side, everything would work out.

Yes. Two people as stubborn as mules, we were going to do it, make our fucking getaway.

Of course, none of this was conscious, but I was fifteen, little star . . . I was fifteen years old and I would have grabbed on to anything to get away.

Yes. I could spend the whole night telling you about this, but since I don't have the time, I'm going to speed up and include only two important moments from this little adventure.

The first is the discussion that we had after his reading the first day and the second is what happened after our "performance."

By the way, are you still there, little star?

You're not dying on me, right?

When you're fed up with my stories, just send me a kit and a stretcher and two nice boys to resuscitate my Francky, and I'll leave you alone, promise!

Hey, don't wear yourself out . . . Swipe them from Abercrombie. That way, no assembly required.

*S*he's dead. Adieu, Perdican!
And then Franck stopped and gestured, as if to say, "Ta-daaaaaa! Stay tuned until after the commercial break!"

And I was waiting impatiently for the rest.

Yes, I wondered how those two were going to manage to salvage the situation again, since the death of a pathetic human being, in those frilly clothes, was meaningless, and a good story, especially a love story, always ends with marriage, and singing, dancing, a tambourine, and so on.

But no.

It was over.

He found it moving. I found it irritating.

He said it was great. I said it was dumb.

He insisted it was a good lesson. I insisted it was a big waste.

He defended Camille, her honesty, her purity, her pursuit of perfection, and I thought she was repressed, too easily influenced, never able to feel pleasure, masochistic.

He despised Perdican while I . . . I understood him.

He was convinced that she returned immediately to her convent. Sad and disappointed, but reconfirmed in her bad opinion of men. I was sure, though, that after receiving a few conciliatory love letters, she would surrender to him behind a bush.

Basically, it was like we were fighting over a piece of meat and refused to let go.

You could say we were wrestling with words.

Excuse me?
What is it, little star?
You're lost?
You don't remember the play?
Ah, okay, wait. Don't move. I'll give you my version and then Franck's and, with a bit of luck, between the two you'll have more or less Musset's . . .

a) (My version) Camille leaves the convent after having heard throughout her entire adolescence the jeremiads of the nuns, who were simmering with bitterness, disappointment, or despair. Either they had been cheated on, or were ugly, or both, or their family didn't have the means to pay a dowry. Sure, there were likely a few who were more virtuous and dedicated than the rest, but they don't dupe young girls. They pray.

Camille is still crazy about her cousin Perdican whom she had fantasized about for all those years, sealed up as she was in her Tupperware. Yes, in love, wet with desire, pining and all that, but as she is really arrogant, she complains that he was surrounded by tons of other girls when he was in Paris, which seriously straightened his handlebar mustache, and she harassed him in every possible way so that he would say, like, getting down on his knees and grasping her woolen petticoat, "Fine, yes . . . it's true, yes, I've screwed other girls . . . but it was just for my health, you know . . . I've never given a damn about all those girls . . . Plus, they were nothing but whores . . . You know very well I've never loved anyone other than you, my darling . . . Besides, I will never look at another woman for the rest of my life . . . I swear to you on a cross . . . C'mon, forgive me . . . Forgive me for having fallen into dark and dangerous places where I couldn't see farther than the end of my cock . . . "

But as he doesn't play along (uh, no . . .) (and yet he loved her . . .) (uh, yes . . .) (but without all that other blather) (uh, no . . .) (otherwise it's no longer love, it's an insurance policy) (uh, yes . . .) (and all that is in our scene), she decides to go back to her bunker and writes a letter to her roommate in which, instead of saying, "Alas, we just don't see eye to eye, him and me. Get out my bowl and my horsehair mattress. I'm coming back," she makes a fuss about it along the lines of "Oh, my sister . . . Oh dear . . . Oh, I refused . . . Oh, the poor boy . . . Oh, what did I do to him? . . . Oh, pray for him because . . . heh, heh, heh . . . I don't know if he's going to recover from it all."

Fine, why not? She had to say something to the gaggle of giggling nuns who would greet her upon her return, except that, bad luck, Perdican intercepts the letter, reads it (that, we agreed, was a stupid thing to do), realizes that she is lying through her teeth, and decides to punish her by taking up with Rosette, the poor little goose-girl at the castle who happened to be passing by at the worst possible moment.

Camille sees them together, and riled up once again, realizes that she truly loves him and that she has to cut the crap, but continues it anyway, and Perdican—who's had enough of the . . . the backside of all of her to-ing and fro-ing between him and Jesus C.—pretends/decides (a contested point between me and Franck to this day) once and for all to marry Rosette.

So Camille loses it once and for all too and lets go of her rosary and her pride along with it.

Ah! Super! They're finally going to kiss after a thousand scenes in three acts, except that, bad luck again, Rosette, who was nearby, hears everything and kills herself in despair. And the rest you know.

So . . .

Good job, right?

They really would have been better off fooling with love, those idiots . . .

They had everything. Cash, beauty, health, youth, a nice daddy, feelings for each other, everything . . . and they destroyed it all, and killed someone while they were at it, on a . . . on a whim . . . out of selfishness . . . for the pleasure of beating around the bush and babbling around a fountain while batting each other on the nose with their fans.

Disgusting.

b) (Franck's version) Camille loves Perdican. It was true love. She loved him more than he had ever loved her and will ever love her.

She knows it because when it comes to love, she is more of an expert than both he and his cock, however talented, put together. Why? Because at the convent, she had encountered True Love, Great Love, Pure Love. The type that never disappoints you and that has nothing to do with the sexual escapades that keep purepeople.com and its lawyers in business.

Yes, she had been touched by grace and she was ready to sacrifice her happiness on Earth to serve her Eternal Lover.

So she has simply come to give her uncle a kiss and get I don't know what. (The dough that is coming to her from her mother? I don't remember anymore . . .). Alas, she realizes that her cousin Didi, even if he is fickle, featherbrained, and mortal, has a real effect on her.

Damn. Everything is turned upside down.

Fine, it's true, she screwed everything up in her hypocritical letter in which she pretended to be a femme fatale, but one, he didn't have to read it, two, he should have come to see her in person instead of taking advantage of that poor Rosette to piss her off (Rosette who, it must be said in passing, is a real human being, with a heart, a soul, tears and . . . uh . . . some geese and turkeys).

Oh how petty is this revenge . . . But there you have it, she loves him. And when she loves, she is direct. Whether with God or with a coward. When she loves, she doesn't stop to work things out. She gives her whole self. And when she got all upset earlier, that's to say, in our scene, with her anxiety about love, death, waning attraction, and loyalty, it wasn't at all to bore him, but so that he would reassure her.

Alas, it didn't work.

Since she's a thousand times more mature than he is and since he's at any rate completely controlled by his dick (how would they have said it at the time? by his halberd with tassles?), he catches none of her hints and assumes she's a poor, exalted Ms. Freeze completely misguided by her mother abbesses.

In short, the little baron isn't playing with a full deck.

But since this is Camille the Sublime we're talking about, she is prepared to swallow heaps of snakes for the sake of love.

Yes, because she is devoted to Perdican, she is even willing to be loved without any guarantees and in shuffle mode. Classy, right? Especially coming from her . . . Because Camille, that's how she is: madness within rectitude. You think she's frigid, but it's totally the opposite. She's all lava, this girl, an outpouring of lava.

She loves crazy love and that's what makes her vulnerable. And also beautiful . . .

Girls like that come around once a century and generally end up badly.

A problem of voltage, you might say.

Since they are too intense for the sockets you find on the market, no matter how much they try to make themselves compatible, each time you turn them on, poof! Everything blows up.

Okay, of course, the electricity comes back on afterward and everyone says "Aaaah . . . " returning to their daily grind, but they are already dead, burnt out. You shake them a bit and since they make a *gling gling* sound inside, you toss them in the trash.

So what's the story with this Camille? Was it her true nature or did she swallow too many holy wafers?

Was she born with a heart too large to enjoy instant happiness or will the lava freeze up again when they're old and she sees Perdicanarian's dirty socks, tossed aside next to her bonnet?

You'll be able to tell by looking at their faces on the day of their twentieth wedding anniversary, except that, game over, this moron of a daddy's boy played too much with matches and poor Rosette—disgusted at being passed back and forth like a hot potato by these two wealthy good-for-nothings who coo at you all day but who don't give a rat's ass about cleaning the mud from their boots before walking over other people—kills herself off in the wings.

Ah, shoot . . . Not only is it bad form but it's ruining the ambiance . . . Hey! Cancel the caterer! The undertaker is taking over!

Adieu lovers, sermons, marriages, fifes and tambourines, the play is over and everyone gets up, their heart a bit heavy.

So here's the upshot of Franck's version: Whether it's Camille's passion or Rosette's act of desperation, it's the same story: Love is total or it's not love.

Because, you should NOT FOOL with love.

Period.

* * *

I'm telling you this in >> x 64, but of course it took us hours and hours to unravel that whole mess.

Plus Franck ended up admitting to me that the author had written this play after an unhappy love affair, like, in order to expose the girl who had dumped him, and that just reinforced the uneasy feeling that all this waste had aroused in me.

Disguised in Musset was a vengeful little know-it-all who was making me uncomfortable. It was too much for my little brain to accept and I didn't dwell on it, but I knew one thing for sure: this Musset fellow, he wasn't very up-front. He used

Camille for his own interests and his interests didn't have much to do with God's love . . .

I didn't dwell on it because I saw clearly that Franck was about to mock me since you're not supposed to mix art and sex talk like that, but I . . . okay, since I wasn't doing well in French, I zipped my lip, but meanwhile, I understood her one hundred percent, the good lady who had kicked Musset out.

Oh yeah . . . Not very honest that poet . . .

So there you have it . . . we argued about it vehemently and maybe we'd still be at it now if Franck hadn't looked at his watch.

"Darn," he said, and he got up because he had to hurry home for dinner. (At my house, the schedule is . . . uh . . . more flexible . . .)

(A boy who says "darn" and who worries about throwing off his mommy's schedule, that's really weird . . . Everything seemed weird to me, everything . . . In reality, I was learning more than just a role in a play, I was learning . . . an entire civilization . . .) (But upside down.) (There you had the barbarian with a bone through his nose dressed in loincloth made from a banana peel observing the Whites in secret.)

Franck had just looked at his watch, and the important moment, the one I told you about earlier, uh well, it only starts now. It's the conversation we had on the way from Claudine's (aka Grandma) (but I was allowed to call her Claudine) to his house.

Since it's very important and I've had enough of telling you everything indirectly with all those "thises" and "thats" that slow down the story, I'll tell it to you in dialogue.

I'll do it the way Alfred would . . .

Tap! Tap! Tap! (That's the stage manager banging a stick to indicate the play is about to begin.)

Whiiiiiiiiiirrrr (The curtain rises.)

Rrrrrrrrrrrrrreucht . . . Grrouinch . . . Frrrrrhhh (That's the sound of old people coughing and blowing their nose.)

La, la, li, li . . . la la (Background music.)

A path
Franck and Billie are chatting

BILLIE: Actually, it's really you who should play Camille.

FRANCK (*acting as though he'd just been bitten in the calf*): Why do you say that?

BILLIE (*who couldn't give a damn about his calf*): Well, because . . . Because you respect her! So much so that you defend her to the end! I'd like to bond with her, but I just don't get her, that girl . . . I think she gets too riled up . . . Hey, it's not a problem learning all the stuff she babbles, okay? It's just that I like Perdican better.

Silence

FRANCK (*in Madame Guillet's tone of voice*): No one is asking you *to be* Camille, just to play her.

BILLIE (*in Billie's tone of voice*): Yes, well, if we're playing already, let's play! I prefer to play Perdican. I find it more entertaining to tell you that if one day we no longer love each other, we'll each take lovers until your hair is gray and mine is white.

Silence

FRANCK: No.

BILLIE: Why not?

FRANCK: It's not a good idea . . .

BILLIE: Why?

FRANCK: The teacher assigned us these roles and we'll do it the way she said.

BILLIE: But . . . But she doesn't give a damn, right? It's the scene that matters, not who plays who . . .

Silence

FRANCK: No . . .

BILLIE: Why?

FRANCK: Because I'm a boy so I play the boy's part and you're a girl so you play the girl's part. It's as simple as that.

BILLIE (*who is a zero at school but who defends herself in the real world and who senses pronto that she's hit a sore spot so takes a playful tone to lighten the mood*): No one is asking you *to be* Camille, my dear sir, just to play her!

FRANCK (*who says nothing . . . who smiles . . . who is having a good time with this funny girl from the Morels . . . who notices that her hair is clean for once and that she isn't wearing track pants like every other day of the year*)

Silence

BILLIE: Okay . . . you don't want to?

FRANCK: No. I don't want to.

BILLIE: You don't want to say with all your heart something like "And what do you know about love, you whose knees are all worn out from having begged too much on your mistress's carpets?"

FRANCK (*smiling*): No . . .

BILLIE: You don't want to cry out to the whole world: "I want to love but I don't want to suffer! I want to love with an eternal love!"

FRANCK (*laughing*): No.

BILLIE (*really troubled*): But for two hours you've said just the opposite. For two hours you've been trying to convince me that she's the one who's right . . . That he's a loser next to her . . . That love is really super beautiful and that we shouldn't fool with it and so forth . . .

FRANCK (*really troubled to see Billie really troubled, but speaking quickly with his arms in the air*): But . . . but it's only a play! It's a game! It's not like we're before a judge or a career counselor! It's theater, Billie! It's . . . it's entertainment!

BILLIE (*who doesn't answer right away; who tries to find the right words; who guesses without really understanding that her role,*

the only true role she had to play, was the one she was playing now,
and everything else [Camille, Rosette, Perdican, God, Musset,
Madame Guillet, romanticism, the romantic life, romantic theater,
the idiots in class, the stinky graffiti, the mean whispers, the groups
of girls who move away when she approaches them, the insults, the
rumors, the gobs of spit that fizzle out in the wind, the groups of
boys that approach him when he tries to move away, the problems
with the art teacher last year, the words that disgust everyone and
that no one ever forgets, the junior high diploma, the end of junior
high, the factory job, the stores all shut up, the houses for sale, the
future with no prospects, the future with no hope, the welfare appli-
cation already filled out, the TV already on, and so on] is, well, real
easy compared to what was bothering her now; who therefore says
nothing; who gathers together everything her shitty life had given
her till then, everything she's seen, lived, suffered, and heard in and
around the Morels, everything it has taught her about humanity,
those people without faith, without law, without pride, without
morals, without anything; those violent people, stupid, alcoholic,
and mean, who keep churning out babies, whom they couldn't give
a fuck about, kids whom they show how to piss in barely consumed
beer cans, to shoot a rifle at barely born kittens or to wipe their asses
with barely read letters from city hall, who have smoked in their
faces nonstop since they were little, who let ashes fall on their kids'
school notebooks, who slap them just for the hell of it and who
make them sleep alone and in the trailer without heat when they
want to chill out or fuck each other to make more children whom
they don't give a fuck about, and so on . . .)

FRANCK (*worried*): You've stopped talking. Are you angry?

BILLIE (*who is not entirely focused but too bad, who goes for*
it anyway and will do it the way she always does it, off the cuff):
No, but it's just, I . . . I don't understand you . . . And I don't
speak for you, actually . . . I say "you" but it's not you, it's . . .
it's beyond you . . . It holds for everyone . . . There are many
occasions in life where you can say what you think and say it

properly . . . say it with words that already exist . . . to use a character invented by someone else to smuggle in things that you too find precious . . . to say who you are . . . or who you would like to be . . . and to say it better than you would ever be able to say it if you didn't already have close at hand sentences that were already so beautiful . . .

FRANCK (*?!?!?*): . . .

BILLIE: But . . . uh . . . don't make that face! You see that I don't have the words! So don't purposely act as dumb as me! It's what I'm trying to tell you, it's that when you have a thing in you that can help you live . . . to truly live . . . something, like, to aspire to and to inspire you until you die . . . because it was there before you and will still be there after you . . . Yes, a thing that will speak about you when you no longer exist and without ever betraying you, and that . . . uh . . . uh, well . . . why do you give a fuck about one's genital apparatus?

FRANCK: Excuse me?

BILLIE: Yes, you understood me correctly . . . What do you want me to say instead? Prick? Cunt? Tit?

FRANCK (*???*): ???

BILLIE: Oh . . . Are you following me or not? You don't understand what I'm trying to say or is it just that you don't want to? Girl or boy, it matters, like, when picking the color of a baby's room, for clothes, for toys, for the price of a haircut, for the kinds of films you want to see or the sports you want to play or the . . . beats me . . . things where being a girl or a boy makes a difference . . . But in this case . . . feelings . . . the things you feel and come directly from your gut before you think of them . . . the things your life is going to depend on after, like, how you see your relations with others, who you love, to the point that you are ready to be wounded, to pardon, to fight, to suffer, and everything, frankly, but what does . . . uh . . . your anatomical form have to do with it, I ask myself . . . and I ask you too, for that matter . . . If Camille's your teammate, what the fuck does it matter if you're a boy in order to play her? And plus it's not even at the Académie Française but in a stinkin' junior high class in a stinkin' town . . . Okay? Why does it matter to you? To say Camille's words out loud, it's the opposite of risky. She's tough, that girl! She can take it! She's even ready to fuck up her life in order to follow her principles. Have you met many others like her? Me, zero . . . So you don't fool with love, okay, but in exchange, assure me, you at least have the right to fool with the rest, don't you? Or, if not, we all should just go to a convent right away, it'll be simpler! Nah, but it's true. It drives me nuts, all that! The whole mess drives me nuts, all the time! Drives me nuts! And your excuse about a girl and a boy, that . . . I'll tell you right now, it's crap. That doesn't hold water for a second. You'll have to do better.

Silence

More silence.

Still silence.

FRANCK: It's not the Académie Française, it's the *Comédie* Française . . .

BILLIE (*still upset that she had to wrack her brain to say so poorly what was so important to say*): Who gives a fuck?

Silence

FRANCK: Billie, do you know why you absolutely have to play Camille?

BILLIE: No.

FRANCK (*turning toward her in amazement*): Because at one point, Perdican can't help himself and turns toward her to say, amazed: "You're so beautiful, Camille, when your eyes light up!"

The conversation stopped there. First, because we had arrived in front of his doorway and second, because whereas Camille had rejected Perdican straightaway, reminding him that she had no freaking use for compliments, I, on the other hand, since this was the first compliment I had received in my entire life, I . . . I didn't know how to take it. Really. I didn't know. So I acted, like, totally deaf so as not to spoil anything.

Then he indicated his house with his chin and said:

"Of course, I could invite you in for a min—"

I was already in the middle of answering "oh, . . . no, no," when he cut me off:

"—but I won't because they don't deserve you."

And that, of course, was something completely different from Perdican's claptrap . . .

That was the blood the Indians exchanged with each other when they cut a vein.

It meant: You know, little crude and illiterate Billie, I understood you, your explanation earlier, and my team it's you.

And that's that.

La, la, li li . . . la la . . . [1]

---

[1] Franck had barely crossed the threshold of his doorway when his father cornered him and inquired, with a hungry look and a knowing glance, about this *young lady* with whom he was strolling in the street.

And neither the son's evasive answer nor his obvious irritation accounted for the father's good mood. And for that night only and for the duration of the eight o'clock news, he shouted a bit less than usual.

In this way, the frail silhouette of a timid and trampy girl—more or less living on what remained of the family social service benefit and who was at that moment walking two miles as night was falling and as Franck served himself another helping of *gratin dauphinois*— had, for one evening at least, stood up to the Grand Conspiracy that was being hatched since the end of the Cold War (Jean-Bernard Muller knew all about it because he was keeping his files very up-to-date) between the freemasons, the Jews, and the homosexuals of the whole world.

So Billie showed up and Western Christianity was saved. (Author's note)

A nd Franck was right, little star, it had to be that way, and do you know why?

First, because he was a good actor and I wasn't. It was no use listening to his advice: I was utterly incapable of performing like he did, of moving my arms and hands, of speaking ostentatiously and pronouncing the words with feeling. And because, at the end of the day, that joystick I had up my derrière allowed me to play the perfect Camille since she was like that too.

She was just as stressed, suspicious, and stuffed into that potato sack dress that Claudine had made me as I was.

And because he was a magnificent Perdican—and when I say "magnificent" you can believe me because it's only the second time I've used that word since the start of my story, the first time being when I spoke about you and your sisters—yes, magnificent . . . a Perdican simultaneously sweet, gentle, cruel, sad, funny, mean, a show-off, sure of himself, fragile, and unstable, despite being sheathed as he was in his great-grandfather's village-policeman jacket, the body of which Claudine had retailored for him before shining the fox-head buttons as if they were pieces of gold. And also because of my two-flavored Malabar.

Let me explain. In the final tirade, the one everyone is waiting for and which Franck had spoken to me about the first day, the famous scene of the scoundrels and the sluts, at one point Perdican says to Camille, clenching his jaw to prevent all his anger from exploding and crushing her: "All men are liars; fickle, deceitful, garrulous, hypocritical; arrogant or cowardly; contemptible and lascivious buggers; all women are treacherous, vain, mendacious, indiscreet, and depraved; and the whole world is nothing but a bottomless pit where the most shapeless seals slither and twist on mountains of muck, and so on."

When we were rehearsing then, we had already been meeting with each other every day for two weeks and through our chats, whether in our roles as Camille and Perdican, or as Franck and Billie, of course, we knew everything about each other and had become friends for life.

So he didn't need to hide from me that something was bothering him as I had already guessed.

Uh, yeah . . . I'm not delusional . . . obviously my performance was totally dragging him down . . .

I wormed it out of him so we could have it out once and for all and then stop talking about it.

"Go on. Spit it out. I'm listening."

He rolled up his book as though it were a little billy club. Then he took a breath, looked at me, frowning, and finally muttered:

"It's one of the most beautiful sections of the play . . . maybe the most beautiful . . . and since I'm the one who has to perform it, it's going to be ruined."

"Uh . . . why do you say that?"

"Because . . . " he said looking elsewhere, "because when I say the word 'bugger' Franck Mumu will take the place of Perdican and everyone will snicker . . ."

I was so not expecting this reply (Franck never shows any weakness and even now, you see, if he passed out, it was to hide that he was suffering), that I didn't respond immediately.

(That too was something I'd learned with him . . . This sly manner that doubts always have of wending their way into the most twisted and unexpected places and especially with people who are made of stronger stuff than you.)

I said nothing.

I waited a second . . . Then another . . . Then another and finally swung myself around to a place where he could see me.

"I'll bet you anything that you're wrong."

And as he didn't react, I put all I had into it:

"Hello? Franck . . . Do you hear me? Look at me, please. I'll bet you a two-flavored Malabar bubble gum that *no one* will snicker."

And damn, I won that bet hands down! Hands down! And I'm crying over it . . . I'm still crying . . .

Sorry . . . sorry . . . It's the cold, my hunger, my exhaustion . . . sorry . . .

I'm crying about it because it wasn't one Malabar he would have owed me but two pounds! A container! A boatload!

Yes, he would have had to bury me under an avalanche of Malabars if he had been brave enough to trust me . . .

* * *

Due to the chronological order of the play, we were to perform last. Kind Madame Guillet granted us permission to slip out to the hall for five minutes to change, and when we returned to our classroom—I dressed only in gunnysack finery with my crucifix around my neck and he, his hips looking swell in his fine frock coat with golden buttons, wearing high equestrian boots—the tide already seemed to be turning in our favor.

Yes, already the incessant chatter about us was clearly starting to diminish.

It seemed that we had won over our audience, and then we simply repeated what we knew completely by heart having gone over it again and again in Claudine's . . . funeralish? . . . funereal?—shit, wait, I'm going to put this in plain language, if not, I'm going to have too many problems—again and again in Claudine's gloomy little dining room.

Except that we repeated it a lot better.

Me because I was as nervous as Camille and he because he was uninhibited . . .

Not caring about the lottery, and who was supposed to act what, we performed all of scene 5 of the second act, which is much, much, much more than had been required of us.

How often can an honest man love?

If your parish priest blew on you and told me that you would love me all your life, should I believe him?

Raise your head, Perdican! What man believes in nothing?

You play your part as a young man and you smile when you hear about abandoned women . . .

Is your love merely a coin that you pass from one hand to another until you die?

No, it's not even a coin; for the smallest gold coin is worth more than you and keeps its effigy no matter what hand it passes to.

Okay. That's it for me. That's all I remember.

And those snippets of worry, or that bit of Camille I have left in me, I repeat them at night and I repeat them for you, little star . . .

How often can an honest man love?
Raise your head, Perdican!
Is your love merely a coin?

It's beautiful, isn't it?

And now that I've grown up and have always sworn eternal love and always forsaken it once and for all and have cried and have suffered and have made others suffer and have begun again and will begin again, I understand her better, that little sweetie . . .

At the time, I had such a chip on my shoulder that I thought she was a bitch, but today, I know exactly what she was: an orphan.

An orphan like me who, like me, was bursting with love . . .

Yes, today, I would perform her character more tenderly.

As for Franck, it was simple. He set fire to classroom 204, building C, of Jacques-Prévert Junior High in the second hour of the school day, that Thursday of April of I don't remember what year.

Affirmative, Fire Chief Clang-Clang: Fire!

He danced around, he jumped, he teased me, he spun me around, he transformed the teacher's desk into the edge of a well, he picked up his chair and then put it back down with a sharp blow, he leaned against the blackboard, he played with the chalk, he spoke to my shadow which took refuge between a cabinet of dictionaries and the emergency exit, he leaped toward the ass-kissers in the front row and spoke to them as if calling them as witnesses, he . . .

He was this seducer, this kid, this aristocrat from the provinces who still bore the scent of the Parisian prostitutes, this oaf, this bastard, this brittle and delicate boy.

And in love . . . proud . . . a con man . . . sure of himself . . . And wounded perhaps . . .

Yes . . . fatally wounded . . .

Now that I've grown up and have and so on and so forth, it's a question I ask myself too . . .

Like Franck, Perdican must have suffered more than he was able to show . . .

In short, when the moment came to dream of my Malabar rather than my virginity, I mean by then, when those words that had caused him so much anguish the day before came gushing out of his heart, when he finally let it rip—that's what we say about mopeds . . . If you want to go, like, four miles an hour faster and bust your ears even more, you say, "Let it rip!"—as I was saying, when it was my turn to listen with more attention than Camille had ever done back in her day, because I knew how much it cost him to say them, yes, the moment when he fired away at me like that (excuse me in advance for the mistakes, I knew it by heart for a long time, but I've surely forgotten two or three things over the years), looking me straight in the eyes and with his hand resting on the doorknob of our classroom, he said:

"Adieu, Camille. Go back to your convent. And when they tell you hideous stories and have poisoned you, answer with this: All men are liars; fickle, deceitful, garrulous, hypocritical; arrogant or cowardly; contemptible and lascivious buggers; all women are treacherous, vain, mendacious, indiscreet, and depraved; and the whole world is nothing but a bottomless pit where the most shapeless seals slither and twist on mountains of muck; but there is in this world something holy and sublime, it's the union of two beings so imperfect and so awful . . . We are often deceived by love, often wounded and often unhappy, but we love. And when we're on the edge of death, we turn to look back and say to ourselves: I have often suffered; I was wrong sometimes, but I loved. I'm the one who has lived, and not a false being created by my pride and my boredom."

Hey . . .

Even you fell for it, right?

So, you agree . . . the word *bugger*, it slid right out like a fart on an ice floe . . .

No one snickered. No one.

And no one clapped either. No one.

And do you know why?

No? C'mon, of course, you do. You can guess, right?

C'mon . . .

Okay, they didn't say anything because they were stunned, that bunch of little bastards!

Ha! Ha! Ha!

Excuse me, little star, excuse me . . . I'm embarrassed . . . It was to hear my laughter in the night . . . To give myself a little encouragement and to say bonjour to the owls . . .

Excuse me.

I'll start again:

No one clapped because they were so shocked that their idiot brains couldn't find the clap button on the remote control.

The worst was the teacher's clap button. It had completely disintegrated into the remote . . .

Seriously, it lasted for a long time, a long time . . . 1 . . . 2 . . . 3 . . . you could have counted the seconds like a boxing referee. We didn't move. We didn't know if we were allowed to go back out to change our clothes or if we should go back to our places in our costumes and then there was a little explosion in the back and, of course, all the others followed.

All of them. Insane. Unrelenting.

As though an enormous firecracker had blown up in our faces.

And . . . oh . . .

How pretty it was . . .

But the most beautiful part, for me, was now:

When the bell rang and they all took off for recess, the teacher came up to us while we were packing up our props and asked us if we would agree to perform the scene again in front of other classes. And even for other teachers and the principal and all that.

I didn't say anything.

I never said anything at school. I went there to rest.

I didn't say anything but I didn't want to do it. Not because I had stage fright, but because life had taught me not to ask too much of it. What we had just experienced was a gift. Now, that's it. We'd put it all out there, so enough. Leave us in peace. I didn't want to risk ruining it or wrecking it. I had so few pretty things and I loved our performance so much I no longer wanted to show it to anyone.

Madame Guillet made little Puss in Boots eyes at us, but instead of flattering me, it made me sad. Well, she was just like the others . . . she knew nothing. She saw nothing. She understood nothing. She had no idea about . . . how far we must have come, both of us, to be able to make them shut their fat mouths once and for all . . .

And now? What did she think? That we were little circus

animals? . . . well, no . . . before I arrived, I was in a crypt and he was in an isolation chamber. Today, we proved to you though that we were free, so great, it's over, go home, but don't count on us to come eat sugar out of your hand. Because for us it wasn't a scene, you know . . .

It wasn't theater; they weren't characters. For us, they were Camille and Perdican, two little rich kids who blathered on too much and were super egotistical, but who helped us out when we were in hell and who sent us on our way during your applause, so move on with your need for a show, move on. We're no longer performing and will never perform again for the simple and good reason that it was never a performance in the first place.

And if you haven't already understood, you'll never understand, so . . . no apologies . . .

"You don't want to?" she repeated, all disappointed.

Franck looked at me and I said no with a tiny shake of my head. A sign that only he could see. A code. A murmur. A sign between Indian brothers.

So he turned toward her and said, in, like, a decisive and super-cool way:

"No, thank you. Billie isn't eager to do it, and I respect her wishes."

And that really hit me with full force.

I still have the mark on my skin and I'll never do anything to hide it.

I'm too proud of it . . .

Because his kindness, his patience, Claudine's kindness, her grenadine that had been expired since 1984, her Pépito candies, her Banga soda, her warm hands on my neck when she was arranging my dress, the silence earlier, the applause to die for, the teacher who had never reckoned that she would do anything other than humiliate me or put zeros next to my name and who was now doing contortions in front of me so she could look good in front of the principal, all that was very nice, and though I wouldn't argue, it was zilch compared to what he had just said . . .

Zilch.

"I respect her wishes."

He respected my wishes.
And in front of a teacher, too!
But . . . for me, certain evenings, it was a struggle just to have something to eat! There were mornings, I didn't even know if my . . . no, nothing . . . the word "respect" was so devoid of meaning that I didn't even understand why it was invented! I thought it was a dumb thing you concluded a let-ter with, like—"Respectfully yours, Mr. President"—with your signature underneath and all that . . . and this guy, this little Franck Mumu who must have weighed 110 pounds completely wet, what did he do? He made the teacher nervous in front of me and forced her to look at me in a pleading way.

Oh my God. It was a big deal.
It was something . . .
Excuse me? What, you fools? You *still* want to get on our case? Oh, well, no. No, thank you. It seems that Billie really doesn't want to and that someone respects her wishes.
Oh . . .
I was born at that moment . . .
Besides, as soon as Madame Guillet turned on her heels, I who never opened my mouth in class, I screamed. I screamed like a wild beast. Ostensibly to blow off steam, but really, I real-ize only now, it wasn't at all about stress that was subsiding or pressure that had to be released, it was the cry of a newborn . . .

I screamed, I laughed, I lived.

So, you know, little star, I'm really going to do everything to try to convince you to help us one more time, but if you don't want to, don't worry, I'll save Francky myself.

If necessary, I'll carry him on my back; I'll grit my teeth and go to the end of the world. Yes, if necessary, I'll drag him to the moon and we'll end up in the emergency room on planet Mars, but meanwhile, no worries, you and all the others, you can count on the fact that my will shall be done.

I admit, I've been drawing out the pleasure but don't worry, the rest will go faster. Note that I don't have much choice, since the nights are short at the moment and I'd better get a move on if I want to finish telling you the whole story before you disappear.

But then, you understand, it's important because it's the show's first season. Like, the one that sets up everything to follow. Afterward there will just be more or less well-constructed episodes that come one after the other until we get to you.

Plus, you know them already . . .

You were there . . .

Yes . . .

You were there . . .

Okay, sometimes, it's true, you were distracted, but I know you were with us. I know.

In the first episode, I made a real effort because I just can't hold back when telling the story of how we met. Those scenes contain the heart of our friendship. Besides everything is there, everything . . . Our way of being, of not being, of chatting, of gossiping, of helping ourselves or loving ourselves. As I said to Francky one day, we're communicating vessels but with mud on the inside, so yes, it was important for me to do a good job recounting how we started out in life.

And that's okay, right? There are plenty of people who produce six-volume works about their childhood and then four more on the first time they used a condom, whereas I've given it to you in one scene. That's the right way to do it, admit it.

* * *

I won't say that everything was easy after that, but there were two of us, so actually yes, I'll say it: everything was easier after that. By recess on that same day, everyone was already calling us Camille and Perdican. Hey, that really put us on a pedestal, don't you think?

Precisely because we didn't want to repeat it, our performance became a sort of mythic thing, and anyone who was absent that day because they were sick or something, according to the others, it was as though they had missed an Olympic competition in which France took the gold.

The miles of ridiculously ornamental sentences that bratty girl from the trailer park just barely managed to perform, Franck Mumu's anger when he explained in a killer voice how a woman tears you apart with love, and our super beautiful made-to-order costumes: it became a big deal. I didn't get better grades for all that, nor did Franck make more friends, but okay, instead of insulting us, now everyone ignored us. So, thank you, Alfred de Musset, thank you.

(Though I insist, you didn't need to do in little Rosette to help your cause.) (If all men who were cheated on did the same thing, there wouldn't be many people left on this planet . . .)

* * *

Franck and I didn't become inseparable—too much still separated us: his really screwed-up father who had transformed his long-term unemployment into a crisis of extreme paranoia and spent all his time on the Internet exchanging top-secret information with his legionnaire friends from

Christendom; his mother who swallowed kilos of Médoc to forget that she was living with such a nutcase; my own father who didn't need a computer to have the impression that he was a type of legionnaire on an official assignment; and my drunk of a stepmother with her pack of male rats, female rats, and baby rats who did nothing but howl all day long. No matter how hard we tried to rise above it, all that shit weighed us down.

Please excuse my vulgarity. In other words, all that misfortune clipped our wings. We were like little birds, dumped in bad nests . . .

Plus, because I was weaker than he, I always tried to join groups and get others to like me, while he was a loner. He was the hero of Jean-Jacques Goldman's song: the one about the guy who walked alone without a witness, without anyone, with his steps that ring out and the night that forgives him and all that.

His solitude was his crutch; mine was my gang of lousy girls.

Once or twice, at the beginning, I had tried to go talk to him during recess or to sit next to him in the cafeteria but even if he was nice to me, I sensed that I was upsetting him a little bit so I stopped trying.

We spoke only on Wednesday afternoons because he went to have lunch at Claudine's house and because, as a result, I didn't take the bus in order to walk a little way with him.

At first, she invited me to stay, but since I always said no, she finally stopped asking.

I don't know why I refused. Always this story about a gift that was too precious to mess with, I think . . . I was afraid that if I went back to that house I would ruin things. Easter break was my only beautiful memory and I wasn't yet ready to remove it from the display case.

You might not realize it because I'm the only one speaking now since Francky is comatose and since, in the meantime, I've learned to express myself but back then, I was very nervous.

Very, very nervous . . .

It wasn't as though I had been really physically abused during my childhood, to the point of, like, my ending up on page one of *Détective* magazine or something, but I was always slapped around *just a little bit.*

All the time, all the time, all the time . . .

A little slap here, a little slap there, a blow from below, a little kick in the legs when I was in the way, or when I wasn't, hands always raised to make like, wait, I'm going to give you a smack and all that, and that made me . . . how can I put it?

One day, I remember, I was secretly reading in an employment contract a thing about alcohol that said, of course, you shouldn't drink, but if you got, like, sloshed one night, it was like throwing a bucket of water on the floor: it's not great, but okay, afterward you mop up quickly, the floor dries, and we forget about it, while alcoholism, even if concealed and under control, it happens drop by drop, and little by little, drop of water after drop of water, in the end you inevitably have a hole in the floorboard. Even the most solid kind . . .

And, well, that's what it was like, little slaps and little bruises that I received nonstop since I was a kid . . . It didn't get me a mention in the news or a file with social services, but it messed with my head. And that was the reason I was so nervous: any little draft of air blew right through me and knocked me immediately back. And Franck, at that moment, he wasn't all that sturdy either and couldn't support me the way I needed him to. So we were very cautious with each other. We liked each other, but we didn't stick together too closely to avoid jinxing it.

But it was okay because once again, we knew.

We knew that between us, it wasn't disdain or indifference but precaution and even though we couldn't show it, we would always be friends.

He knew because when I sensed that he was more sad than lonely or a little more depressed than dreamy, I stood in front of him, and said: "Raise your head, Perdican!" and I knew because even if sometimes he wanted to know or was curious about my life, he never suggested accompanying me to my house. Plus he never asked me questions that were too specific. He was polite, respectful, discreet. As his father would say, he must have suspected that at the Morels' place, it wasn't exactly the cradle of Christianity.

The half-hour trip we shared on Wednesdays allowed us to get through the rest of the week. We didn't really speak to each other, but we were together, and we revisited the good old days.
And that was fine.
It kept us going.

* * *

It was around the middle of June that I started to freak out: I wasn't promoted to the next grade, not even on the vocational track, and Franck, he was going to boarding school in order to get a better education.
It was a period when my head spun from all the anxiety in an alarming way and I tried not to think about it, but there was no avoiding it, it was written right there on my report card: "Not promoted," and on the letter he had just showed me, all happy: "Accepted to boarding school."
And bam! Another punch in the stomach.
That day, I remember, I asked Claudine if I could stay to eat with them and it was dumb because I didn't swallow a thing.

I told the truth, that I had a stomachache, and Claudine forgave me since it was normal for a girl my age to have stomachaches but she was wrong of course . . . It wasn't that type of stomachache . . .

* * *

Fortunately, there was still a nice memory in store for us at the end of the school year: a class trip to Paris.

It was the week before exams, and we dragged ourselves around the Louvre with the idiots from our class. All those morons who did nothing but take photos of themselves and look at the stupid photos they had just taken while there were so many more beautiful things to absorb.

Franck and I sat next to each other on the bus because we were the only two all alone.

During the trip, he lent me one of his earbuds. He'd made a mix for the occasion so I was finally able to hear her—his famous Billie Holiday. Her voice was so clear that it was the first time I understood a few words in an English song . . . *Don't Explain* . . . That one was really beautiful, right? Really sad but really beautiful. We listened to a few others afterward and then it was time for a bathroom break on the highway so he took back his thingamajig and we each kept to our own side of the seat to give each other some space.

When the bus got going again, he told me some things about the person behind the voice we had just listened to. He told them to me in a gossipy way, like in the magazine *Oops*, and of course, I answered that way, too: like, Oh? Yeah? Really? But of course, once again, he and I knew very well what was happening between us.

It was like my dumb explanation as to why he should play the role of Camille: The words I used weren't good but they got the job done anyway . . .

What did he tell me about the very beautiful voice we had just heard, which was one of the most famous in the world, which has stirred the emotions of millions of people since the invention of jazz and which two little junior high country bumpkins were still listening to in the back of a bus snuggling up next to each other fifty years after her death?

Oh . . .

Not much . . .

That her mother was kicked out by her parents when she was thirteen because she was pregnant; that she herself had a very difficult childhood; that she didn't speak for a long time because her grandmother whom she adored had died in her arms; that she was raped when she was ten years old, one night, by a lovely neighbor; that she was sent to a type of girls' home where she was tortured and beaten; that she wound up in a brothel with her alcoholic mother; and that she too had been forced to have sex more often than anticipated, . . . but okay . . . go figure . . . it eventually worked out fantastically for her anyway . . .

That she didn't simply achieve immortality; her life really soared like a bird—a bird she flipped at the sky.

Don't explain, right?

What was nice was that just afterward, on his mix, was *I Will Survive, Brothers in Arms,* and *Billie Jean,* specially dedicated to Lady Day, so that allowed us to more easily move on from her.

Do you understand, little star? Do you understand who he is, my friend? Can you see my little prince from where you are or do you need a pair of binoculars?

If you see him the way I'm describing him to you, in other words, from very close up and without any imperfections and you let him suffer needlessly, you really need to take a little time to explain your reasons to me because I swear to you, I've endured many things in life, many, many things, but this calamity, God knows, I'm already sure I'll find it difficult to go on living . . .

* * *

At the time, I was too dim-witted, but for Franck, Paris was a shock that day.

Why do I say *a* shock? I should say *the* shock. The shock of his life.

He had already been there several times for shows paid for by his mother's trade association but it was always at Christmastime, so at night and in a hurry, and also with his father who spent his time pointing out the buildings and explaining to them how they were spoiled thanks to such and such schemes and this or that Jew (that guy was off his rocker) and so he had bad memories of the place . . .

But on that beautiful day in June, alongside little Billie who believed, unlike Franck's bigoted father, that a freemason was an honest Portuguese man and who pointed out tons of pretty details for him to remember it all by, it completely changed him.

The Franck on the bus ride to Paris and the Franck on the bus ride home had absolutely no relation to each other. When the bus headed back to the site of our gloomy adolescence, he no longer spoke, he gave me both of his ear buds and the scraps of his food, and he spent the rest of the trip daydreaming while looking out the window . . .

He had fallen in love.

The Palais du Louvre, the Pyramide, the Place de la Concorde, the Champs-Élysées, I watched him admiring them and I had the impression I was seeing Wendy with her little brothers when they flew over London with Peter Pan. He didn't know where to look given that everything was so wonderful.

More than the monuments, I think it was especially the people that had really had an effect on him, their way of dressing, of crossing the street any which way, of dancing between cars, of speaking loudly, of laughing among themselves, of walking quickly . . .

The people sitting in front of the cafés who looked at us, smiling, as we passed by, the incredibly chic people or people in business suits who were picnicking on the benches of the Tuileries or who were sunning themselves on the side of the Seine with their briefcases as pillows, the people who were reading newspapers while standing on the bus without holding on to anything, those who were passing in front of the cages on the Quai de la Whaddyacallit without even noticing that there were parakeets inside because their life seemed more interesting than those of the parakeets, those who were speaking, who were laughing or who were getting annoyed on the phone all while pedaling in the sun, and all those who were going into or coming out of super classy boutiques without buying a thing as though this was normal. As if the saleswomen were paid just for that, for smiling at them while gritting their teeth.

Oh dear, yes . . . It all made my Francky really emotional: the Parisians in springtime; they were his *Mona Lisa* . . .

At one point, when we were on a bridge, or more like a sort of walkway above the Seine, and when, all around, every which way we turned our heads, the view was amazing—Notre-Dame, my famous *Académie* française of our rehearsals, the Eiffel Tower, the beautiful carved sculpted buildings along the quays, the I-no-longer-remember-what museum, and so on—yes,

when we were craning our necks and the other country bumpkins who were with us were using their cameras in zoom mode
while leaning on the padlocks that lovers attached to the rail-
ings. I wanted to promise him something . . . I wanted to take
his hand or his arm while he was looking at all that beauty, salivating like a poor skinny dog before an enormous super juicy
bone that was permanently out of reach and whisper to him:

"We'll come back . . . I promise you we'll come back . . .
Raise your head, Perdican! I promise you we'll come back
someday . . . and to stay . . . that we'll live here, we'll live here
too . . . I promise you that one morning you will cross this
bridge like you were going to Faugeret (the name of our local
bakery) and that you will be so busy with your super completely thin cell phone that you will no longer even notice all
this around you . . . At any rate, you may notice it but you'll
drool less than today because you'll be so well-heeled . . . Let's
go, Franck! What man believes in nothing? Since it's me who's
promising you . . . me . . . your Billie who owes you so much . . .
You can trust me, right?

My dear brother, your family and Jacques-Prévert Junior
High taught you what they know, but believe me, it's not all;
you'll know more, and you won't die without living here."

Yes, I felt this terrible need to promise a picture-perfect
future, but of course, I stayed silent.

For me, the bone wasn't out of reach, it was completely
absent from my life. There was very little chance I would come
back here someday . . . Really no chance at all.

So I did what he did: I looked at the view and hung a sort
of imaginary padlock with our two initials engraved on it.

* * *

And there you have it—the last pleasant moment in season 1.

I'll sum it for you in the recap at the start of the next season: we're the heroes, the setting is shitty, there hasn't been much action but there will be more before long, no one gives a crap about the secondary characters, the prospects for the future are zero, for the girl in any case, and the reason all this continues anyway, well, there isn't one.

So? You have nothing to say?
Hey! . . . Are you asleep or what?
Raise your head, little star!
There is one reason! And you know it well since it's precisely because of it that I've been going on and on like this for hours!
The reason is totally idiotic and I can barely dare to say it. The reason is: love.

A fter that it got sadder and I'm going to run through it quickly.
Afterwards, you were looking elsewhere . . .

First there was summer vacation which put a bit of distance between us (we saw each other three times in two months, once by chance and super uncomfortably because his mother was nearby) and then his going off to school separated us completely.

He was far away and as for me . . . during that period, I repeated a year of school, developed tits, and started smoking.

To pay for my cigarettes, I began to fool around, and so that my tits would serve some purpose, I shacked up with someone.

Yes, . . . shacked up . . . there was a boy who passed by, he had a motorbike, he could take me away from the Morels from time to time, he worked at a garage, he wasn't all that nice, but he wasn't mean either, he wasn't all that handsome and couldn't have hoped for better than a girl like me for an easy lay. He still lived with his parents, but there was a trailer at the back of their yard—and that was great because I felt completely at home in trailers—so I brought my bag of clothes and moved in.

I cleaned it; I sat inside and did what he did: I lived stealthily at the back of the yard.

His parents' yard . . .

His parents who didn't want to speak to me because I was such bad marriage material.

He was allowed to have his meals with them, but me—no. Instead, he brought me out a lunchbox.

It bothered him a bit, but as he said: it was only temporary, right?

Where were you little star?

Oh . . . I have to go quickly over these moments from my past because it reminds me too much of the present.

Because, you know . . . I keep going on and on with my story, but I'm waiting for you and feel really cold.

I'm really cold, really thirsty, really hungry, and really not doing so well.

My arm hurts; I feel bad about my friend.

I feel bad about my Francky who's all messed up . . .

And I still feel like crying.

So I'm crying.

But hey, it's only temporary, right?

Suddenly, it came back to me, little star. Monsieur Dumont didn't only teach me that I was from the underclass of France, he made me write down somewhere that you were dead . . .

That you had died billions of years ago and that it wasn't you I was looking at but your remains. The remains of your ghost. A sort of hologram. A hallucination.

Is it true?

So we're really alone?

The two of us are really lost?

I'm crying.

When I die, there won't be even a trace of my presence left behind. No one has ever understood me, aside from Franck, and if he dies before me, it's over. I'll die too.

I'm looking for his hand and squeezing it tight. As tight as I can.

If he dies, I'll go with him. I'll never let go of him. Never. He has to save me one more time . . . He's already done it so often that he's like some hoisting mechanism on a helicopter . . . I can't stay here without him. I don't want to because I can't.

I pretended that I could escape the underclass, but in truth, I never left it; I tried, though. I tried with all my heart. I tried all my life. But it's like a disastrous tattoo, that crap; unless you cut off your arm, you have to lug it around until the worms eat it.

Whether I like it or not I was born a Morel and will die a Morel. And if Franck abandons me, I'll act exactly like my stepmother and all the others: I'll drink. I'll make a hole in the floorboards and I'll make it bigger and bigger until there's nothing human left in me. Nothing that laughs, nothing that cries, nothing that suffers. Nothing that could make me risk raising my head one last time just to get smacked in the face.

I let Francky believe that I had pressed reset, but all that was bullshit. I did nothing at all. I just trusted him. I trusted him because it was him and because he was there, but without him, such a lie won't hold up for a minute. I can't press reset. I *can't*. My childhood is a poison coursing through my blood and I'll only stop suffering when I'm dead. My childhood is me, and since my childhood is worth nothing, with me behind it, no matter how hard I tried to thwart it with all my strength, I was never strong enough.

I'm cold, I'm hungry, I'm thirsty, and I'm crying. I don't give a damn about you, lousy little star, you who don't even exist in my dreams. I don't want to see you anymore. Never again.

I turn toward Franck and, like a dog, like White Fang when he finds his master, I wedge my nose under his arm and lie stock-still.

I don't want to ever go back to living in a trailer. I don't want to eat other people's leftovers anymore. I don't want to convince myself anymore that I am anything other than myself. It's too tiring to lie all the time. Way too tiring . . . My mother left when I was not even a year old and she left because I did nothing but cry. She'd had enough of her baby. And well, she was right, because after so many years, I haven't made any progress: I'm still the same pain in the ass little girl who cries all night long . . .

I forgave her for abandoning me. I was able to understand that she was still a child and it must have been impossible for her to imagine the rest of her life in the Morels with my father but . . . but the thing that keeps me from forgetting her completely is wondering whether she thinks about me sometimes . . .

Only that.

I've stopped crushing his hand—I need to move; I may want to die in the next minute, but I've had enough of having a sore arm for the next second, and just as I'm rolling onto my back, he starts squeezing me in turn.

"Franck? Is that you? Are you there? Are you sleeping? Have you passed out or what? Do you hear me?"

I've stuck my ear against his mouth just in case he is too weak to answer me clearly and also to act the way they do in the movies, like, when a dying old man murmurs with his last little breath where he's hidden his treasure, and so on.

But no . . . his lips aren't moving . . . his hand, however, is still squeezing mine . . . Not a lot. Just barely. A weak grip. But for him it must be a humongous effort.

His hand is too weak and doesn't really squeeze at all, but he is pressing me a little with his comatose fingers. His fingers, in a last little burst of movement, are saying to me: "But you don't see that your treasure is there, you big dope! C'mon, stop crying! Do you realize you're starting to bore us with your miserable childhood? Do you want me to talk about mine a little? Do you want me to tell you the effect it had, growing up with a mother on antidepressants and a father on "anti-the-whole-world"? Do you want me to tell you what it's like to live with constant hatred? Do you want me to tell you what it's like being the son of Jean-Bernard Muller and to realize at eight years old that you would only ever love boys? Is that what you want?

"Do you want me to tell you again all about the bloody war that was waged? The resulting carnage? The domestic terror? So, stop for two minutes, please. Stop. And can we give up on your bogus star there? . . . There is *no* little star. There is *no* sky. There is *no* God. There is no one other than us on this fucking planet; I've already told you a thousand times: it's just us, us, us, and us again. So stop always digging into your shitty memories and inventing your own cosmogony when it suits you. I hate it when you do that. I hate it when you wallow in that type of easy complacency. Anybody can anathematize others' flaws in place of his own, you know? And I hate to see you like everyone else . . . not you . . . not her . . . Not my Billie . . . The world is nothing but a bottomless pit where the most shapeless families slither and twist on mountains of muck, but there is for us something holy and sublime that they don't have and that they will never take away from us: courage. Courage, Billie . . . The courage to not be like them . . . The courage to triumph over them and to forget them forever. So stop crying *right now* or I'll ditch you where you sit and take off right away with my two well-endowed stretcher-bearers."

Oh boy . . . He really sounded angry, huh? You sure are cranky, Perdican, when your fingers come to life . . . Oh boy . . . and . . . uh . . . What's a cosmogony? And what does anathematize mean? Organize by themes? Oh boy . . . I'm going to shut up now . . .

* * *

Okay, little star . . . Come a little closer because I don't want Francky to hear . . . Shhhh . . . So . . . uh . . . to recap: You're there, but it's no longer you, and you don't exist, but you exist anyway, okay? If Franck doesn't believe in you, that's his problem, but I'm used to your company, so I'm going to continue to tell you my little soap opera in secret, 'kay?

'Kay, she twinkled.

* * *

So where was I? Ah, yes . . . in Jason Gibaud's rotting trailer . . . oh my God . . . how it stank inside! A mix of smelly feet, cold tobacco, and old moldy cushions. Well, you could say that I would have gladly swiped a few cans of Oust deodorant spray at that time!

I was there. I was cutting classes. I was sitting on the steps on the side by the shed so that his parents couldn't see me and I was smoking cigarettes.

When my morale was at zero, I told myself my life was over and I could just as well turn on the TV, open the butane canister, and suck out the gas once and for all while watching *The Young and the Restless*, and when there was a ray of sunlight, I told myself I was Camille . . . that I was just in the process of rotting away in a type of convent while waiting to turn eighteen and that one way or another, things were bound to change one day . . . I didn't quite see how, but okay, that's what a ray of sunlight is: something that allows you to close your eyes and believe a little . . .

There was Jason and there were others, needless to say.

When his parents had finally had enough, I picked up my bag of clothes and went off to frighten other old folks.

One day, much later, but roughly around that time, I ran into Franck in town. I know he saw me, but he pretended to be looking elsewhere and I was truly grateful.

Because it wasn't me, the extremely vulgar girl who was hanging around the market that day. Dressed like a floozy, mounted on stilettos, and wearing way too much makeup. No it wasn't the Billie whose wishes he had wanted to respect, it was . . . some sort of slut . . .

Ah yes, you have to call 'em like you see 'em, little star . . . In those years spent in the crappiest of waiting rooms, there was no Camille of the convent, rather a Billie Holiday of the brothel . . .

Of course, I was acting like a slut . . . I knew it . . . But what of it? I had discovered that with my body, I could obtain a certain amount of peace, something to eat, and even . . . even . . . if I tried hard to find it, a bit of affection. So . . . I would've been pretty stupid to deprive myself, right? I didn't love all those boys who made it possible for me to live far from the Morels, but I didn't take up with the worst of them either. And, then . . . between a slut among the rich and a slut among the poor, there isn't too big a difference, is there? It's really just a question of how much clothing you own . . . Mine fit in an Auchan supermarket bag while other people's clothes could fill beautiful walk-in closets, but okay . . . everyone has his own view of things, right? I did what I could and, while waiting until I could do something else, I did it with my ass.

I was obsessed with turning eighteen. Not because I could then take my driver's test and ride around in a Mini Cooper (ha ha) or go gambling at the casino (ha ha ha), but because I knew I would be more relaxed shoplifting at the stores. Before that if I stole something and got caught, they would inevitably call my father. No way was I letting that happen. That was the direct route back to the infernal hovel. So I stole only small items and it took longer for me than others to get respect.

So there you have it. That was my life and those were my great plans for the future . . .

So yes, it was really classy of Franck Mumu to pretend not to see me.

Since then, I've spoken to him several times about that day, about that really strange moment when I was embarrassed and relieved at the same instant and he continues to swear that he really didn't see me. But I know he did, and I know it because of Claudine . . .

Later on, one morning, I ran into her at a café. I was buying cigarettes and she was buying revenue stamps. Of course, she smiled at me and all, but I saw in her face that look of disappointment that she'd had ever since our play rehearsals.

Yes, I saw it. It was quick and very well camouflaged but because I'd spent my childhood on the defensive, I was quite adept at detecting the least little secret thought in the faces of people who looked at me. Very, very adept . . . She kissed me like there wasn't any problem and said, laughing, that she wouldn't pay for my nicotine habit but that she wanted to buy me a lollipop and a scratch-off and that I just had to choose them and then . . . then, she must have seen, under my tarted-up eyelashes loaded to death with stolen mascara, that I was already on the verge of tears since it had been so long since anyone had offered me a gift . . . Yes, she saw, but instead of saying, "Oh, my sweetheart . . . Oh how difficult life is . . . " and "Oh how unrecognizable you are in that outfit which doesn't suit you at all and which makes you look old," she said something that communicated the same thing but in a much nicer way.

Yes, when we were about to go our separate ways in the street, she said something she just remembered and blurted it out like this:

"Say, Billie . . . you have to come by the house sometime because I have a letter for you . . . Two even, I think . . . "

"A letter?" I said. "But a letter from who?"

She was already far away when she added in a half cry:

"From your Perdicaaaaan!"

And I'm crying.

But in this case, I can, right?

Yes.

In this case, I can.

Because those are happy tears, madame . . .

I waited several days before going to see her.

I no longer know what reasons I gave myself, but the only one that was legit was that I was afraid. I was afraid of returning to her house all by myself, I was afraid of going back there period, and I was especially afraid of what Franck had to tell me. Was he going to ask if it was really me, the slut he had seen the other day in front of the chicken vendor? Was he going to ask me how many cocks I had to suck to get a beautiful leather jacket like that one there? Was he going to tell me he was disappointed and that he preferred never to see me again since I embarrassed him so much?

Yes, I was afraid and it took me at least five days before daring to knock on her door . . .

I went there like the Billie from before, that is, on foot, in jeans, no makeup. Of course, for her it was surely trivial, but not for me. For me, it was like happily returning to a happy childhood.

I no longer even remembered what my face looked like without all the muck I had plastered on in order to hide behind it. Yes, I was afraid to go to Claudine's but when I put my hair up in a ponytail that day, I smiled at myself in the mirror. Not because I thought I looked beautiful, but because I looked like a kid and . . . oh . . . that made me feel good, that little unexpected smile.

Oh how good it made me feel . . .

* * *

It was really my name on the envelopes . . . Mademoiselle
Billie c/o Madame Claudine Whatever and so on.
Mademoiselle Billie . . .
Shit, that sounded weird to me. It was the first time in my
life I had received a letter . . . *Letters*, even! The first time . . .
With an actual stamp, an actual envelope, and the actual writ-
ing of a human being.
Of course, I didn't stay. I didn't want to open them in front
of her; I think I didn't want to open them at all. Like my mem-
ories of Easter break, I wanted to line them up in my display
case and leave them unopened forever.
I put them in my pocket and started walking.

I walked without knowing where I was going. At any rate,
my legs knew but not my head. Since my legs were smarter
than me, they took one detour after another and ended up
leading me to Camille's crypt.
I pushed open the old door, squeezed my way in, and sat
down under the little altar like last time.

The oblivion, the calm, the silence, the designs made by the
lichen, the singing of the birds, the wind that shook the rusty
chains, and so on. That made me feel good, too . . . It reminded
me of the little Billie who didn't sleep around with a vengeance
and who wanted to resemble a girl a lot more dignified than
she was . . . It reminded me of a time in my life when I learned
by heart, and easily, emotions that were beautiful and that
made me believe I had potential.
If there were a shrink around, he would have surely given
me a whole speech about how I was curled up there like in my

mother's belly or some other bullshit like that, but there were no shrinks. There were just Franck Mumu's letters and they were even more effective.

I felt good. I forgot my troubles and even slept a bit.

After a while, I ended up opening them in the order in which they had arrived. The first was written on a single sheet and said:

Hi Billie. I hope you're doing well. I'm doing fine. You know, I don't have a lot of time to go see my grandmother on weekends and I think she misses me so I've decided to write to you at her house each week so that you can go see her for me. Thanks for this favor. I hope it doesn't put you out too much. Kisses, F.

The second was an ugly postcard of his town, with the church, the château, and so on:

Hi Billie. I hope you're doing well, me I'm okay. Tell Claudine that I received her package. Kisses, F.

I put them back in their envelopes and felt like crying with gratitude. Because, fine, I was a moron, everyone had let me know it ever since I was born, but now I saw quite clearly what was behind this clever trick. Franck had seen me dressed like a slut and he felt sorry for me so he invented something with his grandma so I wouldn't completely forget myself.

Yes, all that just to make me take off my makeup once a week and go have a glass of grenadine or Orangina in a little house where people really liked me.

Sometimes I went several weeks without going to her house, but he never fell off his schedule. Every Wednesday, apart from school vacations and for almost three months, I could expect my ugly postcard with a "I hope you're doing well, me I'm fine" written on the back each time. So I spent some time with a human who didn't judge me every so often. I never stayed too long because I was too much in combat mode during that period to risk going soft, but just stopping by quickly like that, with my real face from that time, made it possible for me to hang in there until the next stage of my life.

* * *

One day, I remember, when I had just rung her bell, I heard her talking to I don't know who on the phone (the kitchen window was open): "Wait, I've got to go, Billie has just arrived. C'mon you know, that poor kid I told you about the other day . . . " It pierced my heart and I took off, half running.

Shit, why did she talk about me like that? I was sixteen, I was having sex, I was managing without asking anyone for anything. I thought it was unfair. Crappy. Humiliating. And then I heard her calling me from afar: "Billiiiiiiie!" Go to hell, I thought, pretending to be deaf, go to hell. I took another step or two and then something tore inside of me, and I turned around.

Yes, whether I liked it or not, I was a poor kid and I didn't have the luxury of making myself believe otherwise . . .

I retraced my steps, and she kissed me hello. I drank café au lait with her, took my letter, and kissed her good-bye.

When I left again, I was still not doing well, but I really had the feeling I'd grown up a bit.

With all the responsibility it entails.

I didn't just watch TV, give up on school, or minister to boys who couldn't care less about where I came from at that time. I also took on tons of little jobs. I babysat, took care of old people, did housecleaning, and dug up stones or potatoes.

The problem was always my age. People wanted me to do odd jobs for them, but they couldn't hire me full-time. As they explained, it was against the law. Handling their grandfathers and cleaning their toilets was fine, of course, but as for paying me a real wage, their hands were tied.

I didn't see Franck at all. I knew he came back on certain weekends or during vacations, but he didn't leave the house anymore. It was only much later that I understood that he needed me too during those years, and I'm still angry at myself that I wasn't brave enough, or simply didn't think, to knock on his door to get those morbid thoughts out of his head. But really, I was completely off base to think for a second that I could have had the . . . I don't know . . . the legitimacy to come to someone's aid.

It was a time of survival as they say: "It was the time of my youth . . . " Sorry, my Francky. Sorry. I couldn't imagine that it was as hard for you as it was for me . . .

I thought you were in your comfortable little bedroom, reading, listening to music, or doing your homework. I didn't understand yet that normal people could also have problems.

* * *

And then one day things started to happen.

One day and without doing it on purpose of course, my father did right by me: he died.

He electrocuted himself stealing cables or something or other on a TGV line.

He died and the mayor came to find me one morning precisely when I was picking potatoes with a whole band of real Gypsies, in fact.

Even though my hands were super cruddy, he offered me his and then . . . then, I understood that the tide was turning perhaps . . . Yes, when he said good-bye, I turned back to my tub of vegetables, half smiling.

Little star, little star, you're beginning to tire of us, aren't you?

Raise your head, Franck and Billie! Raise your head!

He shook my hand and asked me to come see him the following week. Once at his office, he explained, first, that my stepmother and my father were never married and that, second, the little piece of the Morels I had inherited was worth something. Why? Because it was located high up and interested a lot of people who wanted to install cell phone signal relays or some sort of antenna.

Wow . . . that's what all those letters were that they sent to us for years that we never even read?

Wow . . . I was the sole heir of that pigsty and the mayor was offering to buy it from me?

Wow . . .

In the time it took for it to happen, I had my long-awaited eighteenth birthday, my stepmother and her little rug rats were moved to rent-controlled housing, I got my check for 11,452 euros, I listened to the spiel of the lawyer, who explained to me how much I should put aside for taxes, and I opened an account in my name.

Of course, at that time, my stepmother looked at me with puppy dog eyes and used emotional blackmail to get me to give her some of the money . . . At least half, otherwise I was really an ungrateful piece of shit given all that she had done for me, and how she had raised me like one of her own and all that even though I was the daughter of a slut.

I thought I'd learned to take her insults about my shitty childhood, but even then, even in those circumstances, that word "slut" really got to me . . . Why? Even when you're a little rich, you don't have as much armor as people think . . . I listened to her spit out her venom and perhaps should have felt sorry for her, but my entire childhood, I heard her complain about my presence, going on and on about how I had ruined her life, and how she dreamed of having a massage chair, so I paid for her fucking massage chair, had it delivered to her new shack, and escaped once and for all.

Everyone made puppy dog eyes at me at that time, everyone. My inheritance was common knowledge in the villages; rumor had it that I had gotten a fortune, like, millions and all that, and I let them say it.

Sure, now everyone said hello to me in the street, but I continued to work as before, and now that the age of glorious legal employment had finally arrived, I became a cashier at the Inter supermarket.

At the time, I was living with a boy named Manu, who also became much nicer of course. In the end, he even succeeded in getting yours truly to pay for his car repairs and the hunting rifle of his dreams, and in getting yours truly to believe that she loved him. In short, things were going well. It's a wonder we didn't speak about getting married.

I thought about Camille's friends who cried in their convent because they didn't have a dowry and I thought about how everything on Earth was measured in cash.

Yes, I really wanted to pretend I was happy, but to go from there to asking myself to believe it, that was a big leap.

So I got 11,452 euros.

Okay, I took what came: I had work, a little dough on the side, a guy who didn't beat me, and electric radiators in the little house we had fixed up together; as far as happiness goes, I knew I couldn't do any better.

So, everything basically fell into place, but you little star, you were feeling useless, so one Saturday evening in winter, the Manu in question came back from hunting and drinking (or rather from drinking, hunting, and drinking) half drunk, and he couldn't keep from laughing idiotically because he had something really good to tell me: "Hey, the little queer . . . You know who I mean, the little queer from the village nearby . . . The one who never says hello and dresses like a fairy . . . Yeah, well, they nabbed him, you know . . . yeah, they nabbed him while he was walking alone in Les Charmettes and then they tried to provoke him a bit, that moron, and since he didn't say anything and acted all haughty, well, they took him with them, you know . . . Christ, in Mimiche's van, you wanna know what they did to him there? They sprayed him with the urine of a female boar in heat . . . Yes, you know . . . that thing . . . the bait . . . the product that you put on the trunks of trees that attracts males in heat . . . Yeah . . . they used the entire bottle . . . Hahaha! . . . Man, he was completely soaked . . . And then they dumped him in the middle of the woods . . . Like that, man, there's no way he didn't get it up the ass, the damn queer! Just what he's been dreaming about for so long! Hahaha! Damn, how they were roaring with laughter . . . Oh, the moron . . . Oh, the little queer . . . Boy was he going to have a nice night; he could thank them tomorrow morning . . . Hey, but to do that, he would have to be able to walk, right? Hahaha!"

I remember, I was in the middle of doing the ironing and it was already dark. Fuck, electroshock. There, in the blink of an eye, just like the Incredible Hulk, my true nature came back.

There, my veneer cracked and, in a second, I was no longer the nice girl but once again the angry little outsider from the Morels.

There, I again thanked my father and all those assholes who had taught me how to load whatever weapon was at hand and who had forced me to fire on all those poor little creatures who rummaged around amidst the decaying car chassis because seeing me cry made them laugh.

There, yes.

There, thank you.

There, I felt my true inheritance.

And there, Manu, he didn't understand a thing.

I said nothing. I unplugged my iron, collapsed my ironing board, and put it away in the basement. I was in our bedroom, I put the clothes in his sports bag, I gathered up my ID and other documents, I put on my jacket and grabbed my handbag and then, aiming his beautiful hunting rifle right at the door, I waited for him to finish pissing his beer and finally come out of the crapper.

He didn't seem to believe me, the moron, so I shot off the door, taking a piece of his ear along with it. And after that, go figure, he believed me.

With one hand on his ear, he led me to the spot where they had abandoned Franck. "If you don't find him for me, I'll kill you," I warned him in a voice that was not my own. "If the least little thing has happened to him, I'll mess up your windshield."

We honked the horn and flashed the headlights, and spotted him going along a bridle path.

Seeing the rifle, my expression, and the asshole who was half-deaf and completely terrorized at the steering wheel, Franck connected the dots. He got in the back of the car with me and our obliging chauffeur drove us to Franck's parents' house.

"Do as I have," I told him. "Grab a bag of clothes. And make it quick."

During the ten minutes he was gone, the asshole didn't stop repeating, "But, you know him? But, you know him? But, you know him?"

Yes, asshole. I know him.

And now, shut up. That's what I want and here my wishes are respected.

Our kind and friendly chauffeur then drove us to the city where Franck had gone to high school (I'm not saying the name on purpose but you, little star, of course, you know where) and he parked in front of the police station. I asked Franck to go look for an armed cop and, when they both came out, I surrendered to Manu the rifle I had bought him as a gift. Ah, yes, Mr. Policeman . . . because to keep it now would be stealing . . .

The pig didn't understand a thing. In any case, as he watched Manu's car pulling away, we escaped to the other side of the road. The cop bawled me out for appearance's sake and then hurried back to his pigsty.

I should mention that it was freezing that evening . . .

We went to a crappy hotel near the train station and I requested a room with a bath. Franck was blue. Blue with cold, blue about me, blue about everything. Yes, I think he was afraid of me at that moment. No doubt, when twenty years in the Morels suddenly bursts out of you, it must not be a very pretty sight . . .

I ran him a superhot bath and undressed him like a little boy, and yes, I saw his cock, but no, I didn't look at it, and I plunged him into the tub.

When he emerged, I was checking out a film on TV. He put on briefs and a clean T-shirt and he got into bed next to me.

We didn't say anything to each other, we watched the end of the film, we shut off the lamp and, in the dark, each of us waited for the other to speak.

I couldn't say anything because I was silently crying, so he was the one who had to do it. He caressed my hair very gently and after a long moment, he whispered:

"It's over, Billie . . . It's over . . . We'll never go back there . . . Shhhh . . . It's over . . . I'm telling you . . . "

But I was still crying.
So he hugged me.
So I cried even more.
So he laughed.
So I laughed too.

And I got snot all over us.

I cried for hours and hours.

It was like a plug had been pulled. It was a purge. Or an emptying out. For the first time in my life since I was born, I was no longer on the defensive.

For the first time . . .

For the first time, I felt that finally, everything would be okay. That finally I was safe. And everything came out at once. Everything . . . the abandonment, the hunger, the cold, the filth, the lice, my odor, the cigarette butts, the muck, the empty bottles, the shouts, the slaps, the scars, the ugliness everywhere, the bad grades, the lies, the violence, the fear, the thefts; Jason Gibaud's parents who had prohibited me from taking a shit in their house, eating their scraps; my ass, my tits, and my mouth that had served so well as a form of currency in recent times; all those guys who had profited so much from my situation, and so badly; all those crappy jobs, and Manu who had made me believe that he really loved me a little and that I would have my own house and . . .

And I vomited it all in tears.

And the more I emptied myself, the more Franck seemed to fill me up. I don't know how to really explain it but that was the impression he gave me. The more I cried, the more he relaxed. His face became softer. He twisted a strand of my hair around my ear. He gently made fun of me. He called me

Calamity Jane, or Camille the Nutcase, or Billie the Kid, and he smiled.

He told me about my unrecognizable face, the way I had beat the neck of that poor guy with the barrel of my rifle while he was driving. He described to me Manu's torn ear-lobe, dangling at the corners. He imitated the tone of my voice when I had ordered him to round up a cop and how I had swung my weapon in Manu's face while saying, "Your gift," and he almost laughed at certain moments. Yes, he almost laughed.

I didn't understand until long after, until many secrets later, when he too began to tell me a bit about his solitary war before me, before us, that on that night, if he was so happy to see me so miserable, it was because during the time that I sobbed in his arms nonstop and on the verge of an anxiety attack, he was discovering the first good reason not to die.

My tears, they were his fuel to keep going, and his teasing, that was just to reassure me. To prove to me that we could laugh at it all and that, besides, we were going to laugh at it all from now on since, "Look, Billie . . . look, our lives, as rotten as they are, we're finally here in this rotten little bed . . . Hey . . . Stop crying, my darling . . . Stop crying . . . Thanks to you, we've got-ten through the hardest part. Thanks to you we've escaped. Oh and then if—cry, go ahead cry . . . That will help you sleep . . . Cry, but never forget: of course, our troubles are only just beginning, but when we're on the edge of death, we can look back and say to ourselves: It's me who has suffered and not some false being created by fear and the feeling of terror that some ignorant asshole inspired in me . . . "

In reality, he said only "Shhh" but that's what those "shhhs" said.

Without Franck's kindness during our rehearsals; without

Billie Holiday's childhood, which he had told me about while looking elsewhere, well beyond my headrest; and without his minuscule postcards sent to Claudine's house during my "convent" years, I would never have reacted like such a nutcase. And if I hadn't behaved like a nutcase, he wouldn't have survived either.

So that's it, little star . . . And now, I ask you: Is there any point in continuing? Wasn't that last sentence enough to let us skip the rest?

No?

Why not?

You also want me to recount how it was *me* who got us into this shitty situation so you can weigh it all up before delivering your verdict?

Okay, okay, I'll continue . . .

When I was too tired to cry anymore, I fell asleep and, just as I was nodding off, I made him promise never to abandon me again. Because I did too many stupid things without him . . . too many really, really stupid things . . .

He laughed one more time and a bit strangely in order to hide his nervousness, adding with a silly laugh:

"Okay, whatever you want! I value my life!"

Then, in a really low voice and in the crook of his elbow:

"Oh . . . Billie . . . I had forgotten . . . "

* * *

Hey, little starry . . . Season 2 wasn't bad, huh?

A bit of ass, action, amorous adventures, it had everything!

After, you'll see, it's more conventional.

After, it's two young people getting by. Nothing very original. Especially because I'm not going to be able to go on and on since the sky is beginning to get lighter over there. All the way over there, that must be the East, I think . . .

Yes, I have to hurry up and recount for you the end of the film before the lights come back on.

The next morning, we took the train to Paris.

On the train, Franck brought me up to date on his life: To please his father, he had enrolled in law school and was sharing a little apartment with one of his cousins in the suburbs where the rent was less expensive.

He didn't like law or his cousin and he liked the suburbs even less.

I asked him what he wanted to do.

He told me that his dream was to do an internship that would help him get into a terrific jewelry school.

"You want to be a jeweler?" I asked. "You want to sell necklaces, watches, and all that?"

"No, not sell then, design them."

He turned his computer on and showed me his designs.

They were beautiful. It was as if he'd lifted a lid off an old chest covered in sand and revealed a treasure.

I asked him why he didn't do what he loved rather than obey his father.

He answered that in his whole life he had never done what he wanted and he had always obeyed his father.

I asked him why.

He acted like someone who was busy closing the windows.

After a few minutes, he answered that it was because he was afraid.

Afraid of what?

He didn't know.

Fear of disappointing his father yet again.

And fear of disappointing his mother.

Fear of sinking his mother a little bit deeper in her depression.

I said nothing.

As soon as the discussion focuses on parents, I can't be of help anymore.

So he put away his dreams and we continued our trip in silence.

When we arrived in Paris, he suggested we leave our bags at the baggage claim and tour around before going to his place. That is . . . to his cousin's place . . .

We went more or less the same way as we had during our class trip four years earlier.

Four years . . .

What had I done in four years?

Nothing.

Given blow jobs and sorted potatoes . . .

I was numb with sadness.

It wasn't at all like the last time. It was winter, it was cold, the Seine no longer danced, the walkway was deserted, and the love padlocks had all been cut off and thrown in the trash. People were no longer picnicking in the gardens, turning their faces to the sun; they were no longer chatting away on the café terraces, drinking glasses of Perrier; they were walking just as quickly, but they were no longer smiling. They were all sulking.

We each drank a cup of coffee (small) that cost €3.20.

€3.20 . . .

How was that possible?

I was also afraid.

I wondered if Manu had had to go to the ER and if he had remembered to empty the washing machine before the laundry started to smell like mold. I almost looked around for a phone booth to leave him a message.

It was horrible.

* * *

Franck's cousin may have come from an aristocratic family with a string of names, a long nose, manners, and a Lacoste shirt, but he greeted me exactly as Jason Gibaud's parents had.

Actually no, as a matter of fact. Because of his education, which had taught him to confuse politeness with hypocrisy, he behaved even worse than they had: he talked about me when my back was turned.

For the moment, he said, "Ah, a friend of Franck's. So nice to meet you. Welcome." But in the evening, when I was in the bathroom, I heard him acting all serious as if he were talking about nuclear missiles pointed at NASA: "Listen, Franck . . . This wasn't part of our agreement."

I was ready to leave right then. Because it was true . . . This little Billie was beginning to be a lot of trouble now, she who had never taken the train and who was still thinking about the towels she had left behind.

Wherever I went, since I was born, I disturbed things. Wherever I went, whatever I did, however much I tried, I was always in the way and was punished with a slap.

I didn't hear Franck's answer, but when he entered the bedroom we were going to share from then on (he had given me his little bed and set himself up on a piece of carpet, explaining that all Japanese sleep like that and they live a lot longer than we do), yes, when he entered and he saw my expression, he sat down next to me, took my head between his hands, and said while looking into my eyes:

"*Hey, Billie Jean?* Do you trust me?"

I nodded yes and he added that I should just continue on then and all would be okay. He didn't say, like Jason had, that this was all just temporary, but fine, he could have . . .

And because I trusted him and because I didn't have a job, I went back into servant mode. The boys left in the morning, I cleaned the house, I took care of the laundry, and I prepared a meal for them to eat in the evening.

I loved to cook. I had quickly discovered that the way to a man's heart is through his stomach. I tried plenty of things and gained seven pounds by just tasting to make sure I had exactly the right amount of seasoning.

That all helped His Royal Highness chill out. He acted more cordial with me. Not nice, just cordial. The way those types of people were surely used to behaving with their servants. But I didn't give a damn. I made myself practically invisible and tried to bother Franck as little as possible. And this time I think it worked for me, that defensiveness I always had inside me. For the first time in my life, I was no longer afraid of my own shadow when I turned around too quickly or when I heard footsteps behind me.

I enjoyed the feeling.

In the afternoons, I took a route that passed by all the bus stops so as not to lose my way, and I went to hang out at a big shopping mall on the other side of the highway. I loafed around, pretending to be a demanding bourgeois type who has her husband's debit card but can't make up her mind, and out of boredom, I annoyed the saleswomen, who were really bored as well. Some of them began to hate me and others told me about their lives.

I never bought anything, but one time, I went to the hairdresser.

The girl who washed my hair asked if I wanted a little extra treatment. I was about to say no but then nodded my head. Even if no one knew, it was my birthday after all.

Then, it was Christmas and New Year's and I was alone on those occasions too. I swore to Franck that I had become friends with one of the cashiers at Franprix supermarket—"Yes, you know, the blonde who grumbles all the time"—and that she had invited me over because she was divorced and wanted company for the kids. As I said it in just the right way and even bought toys, he believed me and left reassured.

It was my gift.

At any rate, I didn't give a damn.
The magic of Christmas?
Well . . . uh . . . How should I put it?

* * *

The only thing I began to fret about was the cheap brew.
Because, since I was alone, I, too, began to knock back a few.
The boredom, the isolation, the disorientation, the pretext that all this housework made me thirsty and deserved compensation, with all this I started drinking.
I went to the Turkish grocery store below our place and bought 12-ounce cans of beer.
Then 16-ounce ones.
Then a pack.
Like the drunks.
Like the homeless people.
Like my stepmother.

It was sad.

Really, really sad.

Because I was clear-headed, I . . . I saw myself.

Yes. I saw myself doing it.

Each time I pulled the tab, hisssss, I saw it, a piece of me disappearing.

No matter how much I tried to tell myself what we all tell ourselves: that it's just beer, it's just to quench my thirst, that tomorrow, I'll drink less, that tomorrow, I'll stop, that in any case, I can stop whenever I want to, and so on, I knew exactly what was happening.

Exactly.

It was the education I'd received.

In practically one gulp, I recognized it, that shipwreck about to happen . . . that crappy inheritance . . . My head, my arms, my legs, my heart, my nerves, the entire terrycloth body that had been passed down to me . . .

And what does alcohol do to an idle little country girl lost in a sea of traffic?

It takes her back to her origins.

It makes her start stealing again from the stores at the mall in order to pay for her alcohol without raiding the cookie jar at home.

It makes the security guards notice her.

It forces her to be a cheap whore, so they won't make trouble for her.

It forces her to be a cheap whore, so they won't make trouble for her *and* so they'll have a soft spot for her.

It gains her a reputation.

It makes her hang out with those cowboys from the supermarket in their synthetic uniforms who are convinced they have a little power in their hands and a bit lower down as well.

It gains her friends.

A certain type of friends . . .

Boys who are more welcoming to her than the two she feeds in the evenings, who never take their noses out of their books.

Who make her forget the sulky face of Franck Muller, who, not liking what he studies to obey a father he likes even less, has returned to his solitary mode.

Who distract her from always being the least intelligent one at the table.

And then it makes her start dressing up again in short skirts.

A lot shorter.

And more conspicuous.

In other words, it turns her back into a slut . . .

One afternoon as I was on the way out to see my new friends, I ran into Franck on the stairs.

Shit, I must have had his new schedule wrong.

I was wearing a skirt that barely covered my private parts, a pair of stolen boots, each boot a different size (thanks to the antitheft devices), and my fake Louis Vuitton bag that I held up in front of me immediately like a sort of shield between the two of us.

I don't know why I did that. He didn't even say anything mean . . . Just the opposite.

"Well, little Bill! It's chilly outside, you know? You shouldn't go out like that; you're going to catch a cold!"

I replied with some stupid remark in order to get away from his badly timed kindness, but a few hours later, while I was shut in with a security guard on his break in a trash storage area so that he could screw me standing up against the paper-towel rolls, the sweetness of Franck's voice reverberated with all the rest of it and I suffered in silence.

The guy was nice, we had a good time, that wasn't the problem. I just couldn't go back in the other direction.

I couldn't. I knew too well where it led . . . Especially at the end.

It was then, in those situations, when it would be great to have a mom . . . A mean mom who gives you a harsh look or a nice one who helps you gather up all the paper-towel rolls and the brooms before pushing you toward the exit.

That was what I was thinking about on the way back. That I had to be my own mother. At least for one day in my life. That I had to do for myself what I would have done if I had been my daughter. Even if she were a pain in the ass. A crybaby. Even if Michael had abandoned me in the meantime.

But I could try at least . . .

I'd done many things that were a lot harder.

I walked with my head down, I made screeching sounds on the sidewalk with my pointy high-heeled shoes, I took turns playing the role of mother and daughter, getting all worked up by myself.

I was agitated. In a really bad mood. Cursing internally.

I wasn't used to authority. And damn, what could morality do for me at this stage? After all the suffering it had caused me? All those pieces of kittens I had to bury in secret; all those Mother's Day gifts that I had to skip since giving something pretty to my stepmother would have devastated me; all those schoolteachers who had believed for years that I was inept and who looked at me like I was a half-wit. All those bitches who had mistaken my tenderness for weakness.

All those sorrows . . . All those little sorrows lined up in single file.

Shit, now it was too easy to explain life.

Get lost, you slut!

Disappear.

That you know how to do.

I frowned and looked at myself viciously in the shop windows.

I said to myself no, no, no, and yes, yes, yes.

No.

Yes.

No.

If I was acting out, it wasn't a teen rebellion, it was because to do what I was asking of myself was too hard for me. Much, much too hard . . . I wanted all the rest, but not that.

Not that.

I had proved that I was capable of risking jail for Franck, but what Dame Pluche was demanding of me today, it was worse, more dangerous than prison.

It was worse than anything.

Because I had and would forever have only that in the world between the underclass and me.

It was my only shield. My only protection. I didn't want to touch it. Never. I wanted to keep it intact until I died to be absolutely sure I would never go back to the humiliation of hair that itched and layers of skin that begin to smell like dead hamster.

You, star, you can't understand. You must think I'm inventing ornate sentences to make it sound like a book.

That I'm acting like Camille. All alone and ripped apart in front of the whole world.

No one can understand. No one. Only I can. Billie from her cemetery with the little kittens . . .

To hell with you, little star.

To hell with you all.

The answer is *nyet*.

I will never jeopardize my life insurance.

I got home, I still avoided Franck—he was studying in our room—and I changed my clothes.

I was watching a stupid TV show when His Royal Highness came home from business school with his tennis racket strapped to his back.

Trying to sound, like, a little too friendly, he spat out:

"So? What's on the menu for tonight?"

"Nothing," I said, continuing to repolish my fingernails with a slightly classier color. "Tonight, I'm taking my friend Franck to a restaurant."

"Reeeeeeeeeally?" He said, in that upper-crusty way he always spoke, as though he had marbles in his mouth. "And why does he deserve that honor?"

"We have something to celebrate."

"Do you? And might I ask whaaaaat, if it's not too nosy?"

"The prospect of no longer seeing your filthy hypocritical face, you little asshole."

"Oh! What luuuuuuck!"

(Okay, fine, as I was too chicken, instead I said: "It's a surprise.")

Shit . . . the sky is getting lighter and lighter . . . I really need to hurry instead of making you snicker idiotically along with that other idiot.

So buckle your seat belt, my Taurus in the sky, because I'm going to turbocharge now . . .

I don't have any more time to mess around so I'll give you the end of season 3 at suuuuuuuper speeeeeed!

I took Franck to a Chinese-run pizza place, and while he dug into the crust of his calzone, I took charge of our life for the second time.

I told him the secret promise I had made to myself when we were still kids, standing on the walkway of the Pont des Arts.

I told him how I hadn't dared say it to him out loud, but that it was still there in my head and that it was time to seize the moment.

I told him we were going to get out of here. That it was too ugly, that his cousin was too stupid, and that we didn't come all this way to face more ugliness and to deal with yet another idiot. Better dressed, perhaps, but as much of a moron as the guys from school.

I told him he should find us a place to live, but in Paris proper. Even a tiny place. That we would manage. That our room here was small, too, and that we'd already proven to each other that we could respect each other's privacy. That I had always lived in trailers and that it didn't scare me to live in a cramped space again. That I could handle it. That when it came to a place to live, I could deal with anything.

I told him that my favorite time of day was evening, when I watched him from behind, when he was drawing instead of studying lousy laws that no one respected anyway.

Yes, that it was the only beautiful thing I had seen since we had come here: his drawings. And, especially the way his face finally relaxed when he was bent over them. That Little Prince face that I had loved so much when I was a kid and that I had glimpsed from afar in the schoolyard. His disheveled hair and his light-colored scarf that set me dreaming so much at a time when I really needed it . . .

I told him he needed to prove to me that he was brave, and that he couldn't keep giving me advice, asking me to cut ties with my family, and then doing exactly the opposite with his.

I told him that he loved boys and he was right to do so because it's good to love whom you love, but that he had to get it into his head once and for all that his relationship with his father was dead forever.

That it wasn't worth driving himself crazy becoming a lawyer to be forgiven for his sexual orientation since it wouldn't change a thing. That his father would never understand him, would never accept him, would never forgive him, and would never allow himself to love him.

And that he could trust me on that point because I was living proof that parents could do it: they could wash their hands of you.

And that I was also living proof that one survived. That it was possible to figure out an alternative, to find other solutions along the way. That he, for example, was my father, my mother, my brother, and my sister, and that worked just fine for me. That I was very happy with my new host family.

Then I think I cried a little and his calzone was almost cold, but I continued, because that's how I am: submissive slut or sturdy support beam.

I told him he was going to quit his useless studies and sign up for the internship to get into his jewelry school. That if he didn't try it, he would regret it until the day he died, and also that he was sure to succeed at it because he was talented.

Because, yes, life was as unfair in this as in everything else, that the people who were born with more talent than others had more opportunity than others. That it sucked but that's life: only the rich get loans.

Yes, he would succeed brilliantly, but on the sole condition that he was brave and worked hard.

That at the moment, he wasn't being very brave, but as I was his mother, his father, his brother, and his sister, I was going to chuck all his law books into the dumpster and drive him crazy until he gave in.

That while he was going to school, I would look for a real job and find one easily. Not because I was more clever than everyone else looking for a job but because I was white and legally allowed to work. That I wasn't going to make a fuss. That the only thing I didn't want to do was weigh potatoes, but presumably, in Paris, I didn't have anything to worry about in that regard.

(That was the funny sequence, but it didn't work. He didn't laugh and I didn't want him to since his jaw was stuck in his pizza.)

I told him we had nothing to worry about. That everything would work out for us. That he didn't need to be afraid of Paris, even less of Parisians because they were all dull and all slight, that a flick of the finger was enough to knock them over. That people capable of paying €3.20 for a small coffee would never pose a danger for us. So he shouldn't worry. The fact that the land we came from was rotting in shit had at least one advantage for us: we were sturdier than they were. Much, much sturdier. And braver. And we were going to whip them all.

So that was it, I summed up: his job was to find us a place

to live and mine was to mind the shop while he learned the only profession that he should be learning.

And then, there was, like, such a long and paranormal silence that the server came by to ask us if there was a problem with the food.

And even then, Franck didn't hear.

But I did, fortunately. So I asked the server if he could put our pizzas back in the oven for two minutes.

"Suh ting," he said, nodding.

All this time, Franck continued to look at me as though I reminded him of someone whose name escaped him and it was starting to bother him.

Still, after a few minutes, he said, piling it on a little too thick:

"You're making such a great speech, my dear Billie . . . It's you who should pursue law, you know . . . you would cause a sensation in a courtroom . . . Do you want me to sign you up?"

How arrogant . . . It was stupid of him to speak to me like that . . . Me who had quit school as soon as he'd left town . . .

That was really dumber than dumb and quite shameful of him.

The pizzas came back and we dug into them in silence, and since the mood was tense and he started to feel bad about having hurt my feelings, he gave me a light kick in the shin to make me laugh.

And then he said, smiling:

"I know you're right . . . I know . . . But what am I supposed to do? Call my father and tell him 'Hello, daddy? Listen, I don't think I ever told you, but I'm a homo, and your precious law, you can shove it up your ass, because I want to design earrings and pearl necklaces instead. Hello? Are you still there?

So . . . so . . . uh . . . could you kindly deposit money into my bank account tomorrow, please, so that I no longer seem like a moron in Mama Billie's eyes?' "

" . . . "

So there! Score 0–0.

Oh yeah. I didn't laugh at all, not any more.

Instead, I acted all blasé like Our Royal Roommate, and I let out a *ffff*, spitting my olive pit onto his plate:

"Nah, cash is not a problem. I've got some . . . "

Okay, of course that continued for hours, the little conversation to set us straight, but I took a screen shot for you, little star, because I love this image so much: Franck Mumu's head when he realized that the lousy cuckoo bird who was squatting in his nest for months was really a majestic eagle with golden feathers who held in her golden beak a golden key to a golden future.

I don't know how it would look in a brooch, but in a deserted Chinese pizzeria in the Paris suburbs on a Tuesday evening around ten o'clock, it really looked good.

Otherwise, and this was expected, since guys are very predictable, he really resisted me.

I told him he could repay me when he had his boutique on I don't know what square, where there was some sort of column in the middle, and that I wouldn't forget to charge interest, which would be huge of course; but he proved to be a lot more macho than I would have imagined, and ultimately, I cracked.

Ultimately, I admitted to him that when I had run into him on the stairs dressed like a slut, it was because I was on my way to be screwed standing up by a security guard on his break in a trash storage area against the paper-towel rolls and that if he wouldn't do it for himself, he could at least have the generosity to do it for me . . .

That for him his talent was his hunting rifle, and he owed it me.

And then, of course, he gave in.

"*Your gift*," he said, imitating my backwoods armed-robber voice.

* * *

Time is running out . . . here comes another hurried summary . . .

Well, it's not all that important, you know . . . as far as we're concerned, the biggest part of the journey is behind us.

From here on, there's no point in further details. Our little private *Warcraft* gave us something to do until Francky condescended to finally finish his warm then cold then burnt then cold again calzone, but after that, we gave everything back: the clubs, the axes, the armor, the spiked helmets, and all that crap.

We called it quits. We were tired of fighting.

From that point on, we became little bobos like the others, and fuck, I shouldn't say that word, but I'll say it anyway: and fuck . . . it was good!

Ah, yes, it was good to be as moronic as the Parisians! To get all worked up over a lame city bike, something blocking a delivery zone, an unfair parking ticket, a packed restaurant, a phone with a dead battery, or the opening hours of a second-hand shop posted incorrectly.

Oh, it was good, it was good, it was good . . .

I'll never get tired of it!

* * *

To sum up:

In the course of the episodes that came next, our two

heroes, Franck and Billie, left to live in Paris and lived in the way they had promised themselves they would live.

They moved five times in two years, gaining a few extra feet of space and losing a few cockroaches with every threshold they crossed.

Franck was accepted at his school and Billie practiced various trades, some more glamorous than others, one has to admit, but, by a stroke of luck, she never had to work with potatoes.

Little star, you're too kind . . .

They each fell in love with someone, true love, a love from deep down inside. They believed in it, told each other about it, motivated each other, were disillusioned, made fools of themselves, stumbled, got knocked down, laughed, cried, consoled each other, and ended up learning all about Paris. Its codes, its benefits, and its limits. The wild beasts, the land, the watering holes.

They worked like dogs; they fed each other, dressed each other, got drunk with each other, sobered up together, told each other off, left each other, bored each other, spoiled each other, were rotten to each other, hated each other, cut themselves off from each other, rebooted each other, disappointed each other, adored each other, rediscovered each other, helped each other all the way, and, especially, learned to hold their heads up together.

It's they who lived.

Them.

In the years that followed, they separated from each other several times, but always kept, one or the other and according to the vagaries of their respective romantic crushes, their little two-room apartment on the rue de la Fidelité, which remains, even today, their only home port on Earth.

Except to go on vacation. And even then, Billie no longer left Paris, that comforting city that had become her only family in addition to Franck, and Franck, because he was a good son, continued to take the train to see his family the day before public and other holidays.

His father no longer spoke to him, but it wasn't a big deal: he no longer spoke to anyone except his little group of friends on guard against Fifth Columnists. His mother walked around like a zombie but Claudine was doing well. Claudine never forgot to pass along a few kisses for Billie. And some shortbread cookies, which were sometimes a little mushy.

Almost three years went by—during which time Franck had begun an apprenticeship program in a jewelry workshop located in the Marais and Billie had started coming there to corrupt him in the evenings since she had become single again and worked nights at this time (she was white and could work legally, of course, but you can't dream too much), and had her breakfast while he was drinking his little Chablis at night—sailor's delight. Things were starting to move for her again.

Because Franck was often late, and because the little florist woman facing his workshop was at least two thousand years old, and because she took hours to bring in her buckets, her little box trees, her pots of flowers and all that crap, Billie—who didn't like waiting for a boy for longer than what seemed reasonable—had begun to help the woman out and to close up the shop in order to have something to do. (And avoid drinking a half pint of beer before her coffee, let's say, we who know about Billie's habits.)

And thus, a little helping out led to more helping out, a little chitchat led to much bigger chat, little bouquets led to funeral crosses, a little advice led to a big apprenticeship, a few

Saturdays led to whole weeks, little initiatives led to big changes, big innovations led to little successes, little money vouchers and pay stubs led to a great passion, and voilà, she became a superstar florist.

And it was a foregone conclusion, little star, a foregone conclusion . . .

Billie was born to create beauty despite the fact that everything in her previous life seemed to prove she had no right to it.

A foregone conclusion.

A night won't suffice to recount how our little nervous Nellie had become the cock of the walk, of her neighborhood, of the Rungis market of Paris, the darling of the newspaper editors, of the decorators, of the flower-power grapevine of Paris—it requires an entire book.

Although she lacked family connections, that is, someone to act as her guarantor when she wanted to get some dough from a bank, *mama mia*, she could have given lectures to the daddy's girls of the business schools . . .

She didn't just have a nose for business but an eye, ear, mouth, and chin.

What Billie wanted, God invented for her.

Her crazy clothes (in all weather) from head (scarf) to toe (shoes), uniquely in flower motifs (plucked from thrift shops), her hair dyed in all the Pantone® colors and matched to the color of her dog's fur (a type of poodle crossed with a dachshund, but a lot uglier) depending on their moods, and her old Renault van painted pale green and covered in buttercup plants that the traffic cops no longer dared to ticket for fear of betraying the cause.

It wasn't a question of accounting, but fine, hey, flowers wither when they want to, right? So pay in cash, my friends; here's it's too humid for a credit card machine. Look, I'm not lying . . . the screen is covered in vapor . . . Oh, darn, no luck . . .

Pay in cash, ladies and gentlemen, and we'll put a cloud of for-get-me-nots in the boutonniere for your trouble.

Billie's bouquets were the prettiest, the loveliest, the sim-plest, and the least expensive in Paris, and when it came to conquering the world, Billie didn't have anything to learn from anyone.

Up at dawn, she also went to bed at dawn, and hopped around all day between her buttercups and her pansies, with Doc Martens from Liberty London on her feet, a raffia belt, the brazenness of Arletty, and pruning shears, the safety catch unlocked, which clicked from evening till morning. From afar, you would have said she was the daughter of Eliza Doolittle, when she was still cockney, and Edward Scissorhands.

My Fair Fair Fair Billie . . .

Suffice it to say that from afar you would no longer see in her much from the Morels.

Hmmm . . . a certain business sense, perhaps . . .

The old lady was still there, but she had totally abdicated. She managed the cash and converted it to old francs each evening while her young assistant was bringing the plants back in from the sidewalk. Oh, Lord, those plants really brought in a lot of money—she would live well for two thousand years!

* * *

Okay, little star, I relinquished responsibility for two min-utes because it's difficult to toot your own horn, but here I am again, and I want to tell you . . . I want to tell you *now* since the next season is partly focused on you and seems less inter-esting: thank you.

Thank you for everything.

I thank you and I thank you on behalf of my roommate for

life who came back from India six months ago and is working today, finally, in one of the largest jewelry workshops on the square with the column in the middle. (The Vendôme column, they insist on calling it).

I knew it.

I predicted it for him, one evening, in the Lotus Imperial pizzeria.

I should have bet on it. How stupid of me.

Thanks for my life, for your life, for my lovers, for his lovers, for my fuchsia-colored dog whom I love so much and at whom no one will ever point a gun, thanks for Paris, thanks for my old boss lady who breaks my balls but pays for everything, thanks for my little van which has never yet broken down on me, thanks for the peonies, for the sweet peas, the bleeding hearts, thanks because I no longer drink too much but can have a glass of wine once in a while, thanks because I no longer cry at night, thanks because I always have warm water, and thanks because I work in a place that always smells good.

Thanks for Madame Guillet. Thanks for live theater. Thanks for Alfred de Musset and thanks for Camille and Perdican.

And thanks for Billie Holiday who also sang *No Regrets*.

And, above all, thanks for him.

Thanks for Franck Mumu from Prévert.

Thanks for Franck Mumu who was there.

Thanks for giving him to me.

For all of this, little star, *merci*.

And now that all has been said and done, unload your fucking stretchers, goddamn it! I'm freezing my ass off and you're almost gone!

It's true! What the hell are you doing for Christ's sake?

You don't think we've suffered enough?
Goddamnit! Twinkle a little!
Shimmer! Sparkle! Let yourself go!

I know, I know . . .
I know what you want . . .
You want me to look to the sky and say that I screwed up
and that I deserve to suffer a little bit more this night.
Okay, let's get to it, girl . . . let's go.
Turn the page.

Look, little star, I've put on my Sunday best and my polished shoes, and I come to you as I do to confession.
Don't pay any attention to my hair, which is a bit lilac in color these days, but focus only on my pure heart.
A Madonna lily . . .
(*Lilium candidum.*)

If I'm here, withering, wilting, freezing my bulb off, and begging you during the night to help us one more time, it's because I did a foolish little thing.

Ah yes . . . It happens once and a while . . . imagine.

Usually, it's when I drink too much Ti' punch and rum made the way they do it at Samy's Beach Bar, but at that time, I was on as much of an empty stomach as one can be when one has to put up with a family hiking trip, with jackasses and morons, in Cévennes National Park.

What was I thinking?

What was I thinking? What was I thinking? What was I thinking?

Do I regret this foolish little thing?

No.

I even think I should have hit him harder.

You see, I'm admitting everything to you . . .

And if you don't pardon my urges, at least take my honesty into consideration.

Because like Billie Holiday and for the same reasons she
had: I have no regrets.

I have no regrets, and I will never regret anything in life
because too big a piece has already been snatched from me. A
piece that was supposed to be nice too . . . So, no, don't count
on me to lick your Boötes.

I wouldn't know how.

I've never done it.

When someone pushes me into a corner, I prefer to pick up
a rifle or hit them hard.

I'm not proud of it, but there it is. That's how I am and I
already know I won't change.

Since I was born, I've held on only by my will to hold on
and the first person who lays a hand on the things that support
me, as fragile as they are, I'll demolish him.

At the moment, it turns out that my preferred support is
not very strong. He's stretched out next to me; he is suffering
and no longer answers when I speak. If you don't help me to
fix him, I'll make you disappear, too. I'll arrange things
between me and myself so that I never see you again.

You, you don't give a damn, you're already dead, but as for
me, I still have a chance, I'll have you know.

I know how to load a weapon and shoot down a timid animal. So, as far as I'm concerned, I won't have a single worry
about my future without him.

Not a one.

That's it. Everything's been said.

Now I can amuse myself a bit again and tell you about our
super vacation . . .

It all began at a bar in a luxury hotel.

For years, when it comes to Franck and me, almost everything has begun at a bar in a luxury hotel.

Since we work like dogs, we tend to end up in quiet places where everything is order and beauty, rich, calm, and pleasurable.

I no longer faint when I see the drink prices on the menu because I no longer look at them.

I rarely sleep more than six hours a night and can no longer afford to be cheap.

I make it possible for people to deliver pleasure (to themselves) by sending very pretty flowers (to themselves) six days out of seven from eleven A.M. until nine P.M., and to reward myself for having become this priceless treasure of good deeds, I sprawl in the spongy armchairs on the seventh day and offer to my poor friend, the repairer of tiaras and diadems of queens turned to dust, cocktails that are worth a thousand times more than the skin on my ass.

I love it.

I have a score to settle with my past and I'm paying cash on the barrelhead in a five-star luxury hotel. So it all balances out.

I no longer remember what hotel we were at nor what we were drinking, but it must have been really enjoyable since I ended up giving in to his whim.

Franck was interested in a ravishing young man who was

leaving to go hiking with his "friends" (already, I didn't like the word . . .) and their children in the Cévennes and who had suggested that he join them.

The scenery would be sublime, the food more natural than nature, the skies beyond compare, and the pack donkeys just too sweet.

And it would do them good to walk a bit, to get some exercise, to get some fresh air and all that.

Fine.

Franck wanted to go fuck out in the open in a healthy, familial, zoophilous atmosphere, why not?

"No," he said, getting annoyed. "You don't get it. It's not what you think. That guy there, I really have the feeling he's the one for me and I'm not going with him to have sex but because I'm romantic."

Fine.

I've already seen a few men who were the one for him go by; what's one more jackass? I stopped snickering.

As if things weren't bad enough, he wanted me to accompany him on his man-hunting expedition. Like a chaperone. Like a maid of honor. Like, to show his bona fides and that he had the best intentions. Like, to show he had a family . . .

Oh boy, I said.
Me?
Walk?
In those big clodhoppers that weigh a ton?
And a sun hat on my head?
With a flask?
And one of those waterproof fluorescent jackets?
And a fanny pack?
And mosquitoes?
And people I don't even know?

And donkeys that I wouldn't even know how to keep on a leash?

Oh boy, I concluded. Zero chance of that happening!

But in the end, I said yes anyway.

Francky knows what to do to soften me up and the cocktails did the rest. Plus it was a part of the hotel-room-and-hunting-expedition deal: we rarely ask favors of each other, but those that are really important to us, we don't even have to ask each other.

And then I thought: it would be off-season in my little boutique and it would do me good to take it easy for a few days. So, okay, you're on: we went to the Au Vieux Campeur sporting goods store the following Monday and I was soon wearing a type of Moon Boot in undressed calfskin leather on my feet.

It was all way too beautiful . . .

I had decided to approach this adventure like a joke and I started there, in the store. I was a totally annoying customer, trying on everything without making up my mind for hours.

Franck wanted a jackass; he would have one.

To be honest, I was very happy to go on vacation with him. For years we were like two ships passing in the night, and I missed him. I missed us.

Also, it was exactly ten years after our Alfred de Musset rehearsals and I liked that. The thought of getting his goat for a week among the sheep was a nice anniversary gift.

Ten years. Ten years since we had drooled over love. And, in my case, I have no illusions: that was already the greatest love story I will ever know . . .

In retrospect, there was already trouble brewing with this hiking trip as soon as we arrived for our rendezvous at the Gare de Lyon.

That's right. Arthur may have been the one for my Francky, but I had the distinct impression that it was me, rather, whom he was trying to excite on the platform.

Ha, ha, I snickered beneath my sun hat, bad choice, my fey little darling, bad choice . . .

Fine.

I acted like I was frigid and said nothing.

First of all, one can swing both ways, the train doesn't go in only one direction; and second, I was in old-maid mode at that moment of my life.

I was too behind in my bookkeeping to allow myself to flirt with the first tease who came along. So they could sort it out between themselves, Franck and Arthur. I was staying out of it.

Shit, is this a vacation or what?

So, good friend that I am, I quickly discouraged little Arthur in his Ray-Ban aviators and let the boys have two seats next to each other facing forward on the train.

And I slept the whole trip.

Seriously, the thought of traipsing across rocky terrain with those clodhoppers on my feet was already wearing me out.

Then we were taken to a super lodge that was super family-friendly with plenty of other super bobos who were super excited to hike with super donkeys that were super small and super chunks of bread and super cheese and then, right away, I shut down and became defensive again.

Hey, not like when I was a kid, okay? No, no! It had nothing to do with that! It was simple: I was accompanying Franck and that's it. I hadn't come to be subjected to all that conviviality.

I was a businesswoman who did business all year long and now I especially needed to unplug from human relationships. And especially the nice ones.

I wasn't in a huff; I was just taking a break.

It was just too much of a family vibe for me to handle all at once, and I already knew I didn't have what it took to guarantee that I would share in the general enthusiasm.

You Franck, me Billie. Me come with you, you don't ask for more.

Since he loved me and knew me well, he left me alone.

We slept in the same tent, and the second evening, he admitted that he had told everyone not to get upset if I was so taciturn . . . that it was because I was getting over a big heartbreak . . .

I answered that it was good he told them that, seeing as I was always more or less getting over a big heartbreak, and a few seconds of smiles later, I couldn't stop myself from adding that it was even the story of my life, wasn't it? And then we giggled in our sleeping bags to make it seem like I was just too much of a hoot.

I adored sleeping in that little tent with him (I had done a good job dividing up the tasks: I threw the tent in the air (2 seconds) and he folded it back up (2 hours)), I took out my flask of hooch and we told each other lots of things. We said bad things about the group, we snickered, we giggled, we were nasty, we recounted our lives to each other, the little bits of each other's soap opera that we had missed, our laurels, our purchase orders, our stories of work, rings, clients, and bracelets.

Franck also imitated for me certain hiking chants that were even more ridiculous than the others and I laughed like a hyena.

I laughed so much that at times our tent was on the verge of flying away. The others must have thought I'd gotten over my big heartbreak really quickly . . .

Oh, I didn't give a damn.

I don't give a damn about others . . . I only like the people I like.

And my dog.

At one point, we were separated into three groups—something about fragile trails—and we joined up again with some "newcomers" which included a prim and proper family, with their hair neatly clipped about the ears.

Despite the fact that the boy and two little girls were very well behaved, their parents acted like lunatics, always ready to apply the principles they'd read about in the Great Infallible Teachers series. (Infallible, hot damn, I finally got that word right! 10 points! 10 points for Billie who speaks proper!)

They still had their Anti-Gay Marriage stickers on their backpacks and asked me and Franck if we were engaged and if we were getting married soon.

Poor, poor wretches.

Franck, busy with the food, didn't hear the question, so I answered that we were brother and sister.

Oh yeah . . . I wanted to continue to howl with laughter every night in my little yurt with the little squirt without them coming to drop a bucket of cold water on our backs.

We walked behind them and with my chin I indicated the infamous sticker to Franck to make him laugh, but he was a bit perturbed and didn't react.

His Arthur had run off with another group of Invisibles where there was a little twenty-year-old Selena who was unbelievably stupid but whose image made too pretty a reflection in Arthur's mirrored sunglasses and that made Franck a bit disappointed in life . . . "Don't worry," I said to him poking him in the ribs: "You have me . . . " and since that didn't soothe him, I took out my first aid kit:

"What advice will you give me on the day when I see that you no longer love me?" I asked him.

"I'll tell you to take a lover," he retaliated.

"And what will I do when my lover no longer loves me?" I continued to press him.

"You'll take another one."

"And how long will this go on for?"

"Until your hair turns gray, and mine white," he said smiling.

And we were at it again. After that, he perked up.

Long live Alfred!

We didn't have a donkey because we didn't have kids.

The Crewcut family did have kids so they had a little gray, ridiculously cute donkey who was called Donkster. (Super original.) I was afraid of him, but I liked him all the same.

(As for Franck, the way these anti-gay-marriage types saw it, he was so far from having a husband or a family or children or dignity or respect or forgiveness or paradise that a donkey wasn't even worth thinking about.)

Donkster . . .

I called him my little Dollster and every now and then I secretly slipped him stuff to eat.

Mr. Crewcut gave me a dirty look since the rules clearly specified that the animals should *never* be fed while they are working.

It was the number one rule, which Mr. Rent-A-Donkey made very clear: you can give them as much food as you want when they have their saddles off, but otherwise not a blade of grass. Otherwise . . . otherwise, I don't remember . . . otherwise it throws off their GPS, I think.

When I finished an apple, was I going to throw the core to the ants when there was this sweet little Donkster who had been ogling it for fifteen minutes?

I don't do such dumb things.

Trouble was brewing between Mr. Crewcut and me.

I no like the way he spoke to his wife (like she was an idiot), and I no like the way he spoke to his children (like they were idiots). (When I get angry, I speak like that, okay?) (Once the Morels are bred in the bone, they remain in one's mouth.) (Alas.)

He kept sniffing at Franck because he was beginning to doubt that he was a real man, as they say, and that really riled me up. His way of sniffing his ass as though Franck were a dog; it really disgusted me.

Plus he had a real gift for ruining all the nice moments. If the little girl picked a flower to give to her mommy, it was a big deal because it was an endangered species. If the kid wanted to look through the binoculars, he had to wait because his hands were too dirty. If he was hungry, the answer was no, he couldn't eat now, because it wasn't snack time. If he wanted to lead the donkey, the answer was no because he might let it escape. If he wanted to skip stones, he would never succeed because he didn't put enough effort into it. (Effort . . . To put effort into skipping stones . . . what an asshole . . .)

If the other little one went behind the donkey again, she

might get kicked, which could kill her. (My Dollster . . . what nonsense . . .). If the wife said the view was beautiful, he answered that it was better on the other side of the hill; if she took a photo of her kids, he predicted it would come out badly since it was backlit and if she agreed to carry the little girl, he raised his eyes to the sky, reminding her that it wasn't a good idea to give in to their every little whim.

Okay.

I slowed down and to cool myself off, I acted like someone who was really interested in the flora and fauna.

Go have your tantrum far from my donkey, you dirty little kapo. I'm looking at the grasses I will put in my bouquets . . .

When it came time to picnic, he sat next to Franck to make like they were pals and he asked straight out if we wanted to have kids, too.

Francky threw me a look that said: please, don't get involved, and he answered with an evasive bit of bullshit to put an end to the discussion.

While we were arranging our bags on Dollster's back, he whispered in my ear:

"Hey, Billie, don't make trouble with that guy. One of my work colleagues whom I like a lot is in the other group and I don't want a scandal, okay? Like you, I'm on vacation."

I nodded my head.

And I calmed down.

For him.

In the evening, in the shelter of the tent, he made walking sticks for the children with his lovely knife.

He is a chiseler without equal, and when he had finished he handed each of them a little jewel of a stick and their smiles were too adorable.

They each got one with their initials and a personal symbol carved in the bark. For the boy, a sword and for the girls, a star and a heart.

I threw a hissy fit so I got one too. A stick longer and fatter with an artistic *B* and the head of my dog just below it. When he presented it to me, I had exactly the same smile as the little ones, but a lot more childlike.

Then we slept like dormice.

The next morning, I was in a good mood again.

Take note, little star, I didn't have much choice because the scenery was really beautiful.

Nothing can resist so much beauty . . . and especially not human stupidity . . . so all was well. Since he saw that I was relaxed, Franck relaxed too and since we didn't have the right to a little donkey because we lived in sin, we went ahead of the group so the other spoilsport wouldn't irritate us.

After all, we each have to live our own lives, right?

Yes, of course . . .

Our own lives . . .

God is wise and will sort the good ones out.

Right then we ran into a huge flock of sheep. Okay, in the beginning, it was fine, but after a while, I'd had enough of them.

If you've seen one sheep, you've pretty much seen them all; there's not much difference. I was pulling Franck by the sleeve to get back on the hiking trail, but then Bam! Jesus!

My Francky was struck by lightning.

Vision. Apparition. Revelation. Fulguration. Palpitation. Consternation.

The shepherd.

Seriously, I swear, he really looked like Jesus Christ, and he was way too sexy.

Beautiful, smiling, tanned, copper-colored, golden, slender, muscular, bearded, curly haired, cool, calm, radiant, bare chested, in a short loincloth with leather sandals and a knotted stick.

Franck was salivating like the wolf in the Tex Avery cartoons, right in the middle of a flock of sheep.

It was divine to see . . .

Hey, I was also eager to receive communion directly from God!

We chatted a bit . . . well . . . we tried to chat rather than stare.

Franck asked him if the solitude wasn't too unbearable (the little flirt . . .) and I asked tons of questions about his dogs and then we saw our friends the Crewcuts and Co. off in the distance so we said good-bye to the shepherd and went to join them without really joining them, because we were afraid of getting lost.

Just before that, we asked him where he was going and he indicated a little mountain nearby.

Okay, good-bye then . . .

O! Lord . . . how cruel You are with Your flocks! Mass is over, but it was really too short!

It goes without saying that I kept on teasing Francky about it in the hours that followed.

When it came time to picnic, Mr. Crewcut asked him if he wanted some sausage.

"Only if you put it in a shepherd's pie!" I answered and that made me giggle nonstop for at least two minutes.

Sorry.

I apologize a thousand times.

Mrs. Crewcut started to worry and Franck told her, sighing, that I was allergic to pollen.

And that started me giggling for two minutes more.

Aaaah . . . I was beginning to really like this little outing!

Franck pretended to lose his patience but he was happy too . . .

We both knew where we had come from and each time we saw the other happy, we enjoyed it for the other person, we enjoyed it ourselves, and we also enjoyed it because we had triumphed over the crappy hand we were dealt.

To celebrate, I waited until Mr. Anti-Gay Marriage went off to take a piss and I gave an entire apple to my little Dollster.

He gulped it down right away and to thank me, he planted a kind of big warm and fuzzy kiss on my neck.

Ooooh . . . I was already beginning to miss him . . . Plus, in front of my boutique with a straw hat with two holes and baskets filled with flowers on his back, he would have looked way too classy.

So, there you have it, little star . . . Everything was going well and if it all went downhill, it really wasn't our fault, seeing as we had been seriously touched by grace and were walking on water.

We were transfigured.

We were adoring our trip in the Cévennes.

We were a-dor-ing it.

We were as different as we could possibly be from the little sheep we had been.

The picnic finished, we decided to take a break because it was really hot and the little girl had fallen asleep in her mommy's arms.

(I know, I shouldn't say it . . . there's no point . . . no point at all . . . but really . . . I felt a bit strange . . .)

I know I'll never have kids. And that's not just a silly turn of phrase. It's an absolute certainty. I don't want any. That's all. But when I saw the face of this woman who was looking at her little darling and how she arranged herself to keep the girl in the shade by wriggling her hips however she could and by scraping her butt under that tree all while being really careful not to wake her I couldn't stop from telling myself that my mother must have been really sick in the head . . . really sick . . . since I had been even smaller than that . . .

(Okay, forget it, it's not important.)

To stop thinking about it, I turned sideways and nodded off on my Francky's stomach.

To hell with you, Life!

I don't know if it was because I was tired from the hike, or because of the shepherd's belly, or because of the scene of Mother and Child, but I slept badly that night . . .

In fact, I didn't sleep at all.

And poor Franck suffered too. Since I'm selfish and didn't want to be all alone with my insomnia, I tried to prolong the conversation. And of course, like a rat stuck in a maze, babbling in circles, I finally got to the point and muttered in the dark that I was not even four years old but only eleven months and that really, I didn't understand . . .

He was annoyed. I think he had gone off to fondle himself all night while praying to Jesus, so he pushed me away.

So I slept even less and he slept less too.

So there you have it, little star . . . You see, I'm already beginning to set the stage: when we took up the trail again that morning to go meet up with the rest of the group on the plateau whose name I no longer remember, the vacation snapshot was already a bit dog-eared . . .

It was the first time in my life that I had been confronted with a mommy in action, and a nice one too, and that had a bad effect on me. I said nothing and continued to act as ditzy as before, but I felt something deep inside me that was beginning to send out distress signals.

Instead of looking at the sky, the sun, the clouds, the beautiful scenery, the butterflies, the flowers, and the stone cottages, I was obsessed with that woman.

I listened to the sound of her voice, I looked at where she put her hands on the body of her children (always the sweetest spots: the neck, the hair, the cheeks, the chubby part of the little calves), what she fed them, how she answered their questions, how she never made a mistake with their names, and that way she had of always discreetly checking on them out of the corner of one eye . . . it was killing me.

All that tenderness was killing me . . . All that injustice . . . That enormous hollow lack that jumped into my mouth each time I turned my head toward her . . .

So I clung to Franck like a leech but since I got the sense I was bothering him, I banished myself to a corner of the tent.

After lunch, since I was still feeling down, I asked if I could lead the little Donkster.

So that I might get over at least *one* of my anxieties . . .

Sergeant Crewcut let me take over, firing off a thousand ridiculous warnings (like he was entrusting me with a pitbull on amphetamines who had not eaten anything for a week, and so on) and to take my mind off things, I threw myself into a diabolical seduction plan.

I whispered in Donkster's big ear that rattled with pleasure: "Are you sure you don't want to come to Paris with me? I'll slip you all my faded roses to munch on and I'll take you to flirt with the little female donkeys in the Luxembourg Gardens . . . Plus I'll pick up your droppings, I'll put them in way too cute little jute canvas bags and I'll sell them for a fortune to all the losers who make lousy vegetable gardens on their balconies.

"Go on, say yes . . . you're not sick of carrying our stuff? You don't want to live a beautiful life? I'll dye your mane blue lavender and we'll go drink mojitos on the Champs Élysées.

"Because I noticed that you really like mint leaves, right, my little friend?

"Go on, my Dollster . . . Don't be stubborn . . . "

His big sweet eyes looked at me gently. He didn't look opposed to the idea and rubbed himself on my arm from time to time to drive off the flies and to force me to continue to make him bray again a little with all my foolishness.

So I felt better.

I felt better and didn't pay any attention to Mommy Crewcut's sweetness and to her husband's phenomenal stupidity.

You see, little star, it wasn't premeditated at all. The day before, I had swallowed that dirty little piece of the Morels that had stopped me from living, and there was no hatred left in me.

I hope you believe me.

You have to believe me.

I always tell the truth to you and Franck.

* * *

Okay, you're ready?

Okay. I'll tell you everything then . . .

At one point, the little boy who had dreamed about it for days and nights, again asked if he could lead the little donkey, too.

His father said no and I said yes.

Exactly at the same time.

And then came a big lull in the conversation.

"It's okay," I said, "he's completely calm and totally gentle . . . Look, I was super afraid and then everything went fine . . . If you want, I'll stay right behind your son in case there's a problem, okay?"

Mr. Crewcut was really pissed but he had to give in because everyone was saying I was right, that our donkey was not a donkey but a lamb and that he should trust the children and all that.

HeilHitler finally relented, but we had the feeling he was placing his kid in the sights of his pump-action shotgun so it wasn't in the little one's interest to screw up.

Lovely.

The kid was so happy. Like, Ben-Hur at the steering wheel of his Lamborghini, you might say.

As promised, I kept behind him, and like his mommy, sometimes, I discreetly touched his hair.

Just like that.

To see . . .

And, since everything was going well, we finally all relaxed.

About a half hour later, he announced that he'd had enough of leading Donkster and wanted to return him to me so he could go back to looking for fossils.

"No way," his father retorted, only too happy to be able to regain his authority in the eyes of the group. "You wanted to lead him, well, now you have to carry through. You need to learn that we make choices in life, my dear Antoine. You decided to be responsible for this animal, very well, so now you be quiet and lead him until we get to the camp, got it?"

This bullshit again?

Oh, oh . . . I was really going to have to get mixed up in this conversation.

Oh, oh . . . where are you, my Francky?

Don't stay too far behind, sweetie, because I'm getting the feeling my shirt is about to burst . . .

And I look a little green about the gills, don't you think?

So this little Antoine, who was super cute, a super good walker, super happy, super brave, super easygoing, super affectionate, and super sweet with his little sisters, began to whimper, calling for his mother.

And then his father gave him a mean little slap behind the head to teach him a lesson.

Oh, fuck . . .
Oh, I recognized it . . .
I recognized it because I know it by heart.
It was the worst.
The weakest of the weak.
The most vicious.
The most painful.
The kind that doesn't leave a mark but detaches you from your cerebellum in a second.
The kind that gives you whiplash inside.
The kind that no one ever suspects and that so shakes your cranium, making you unable to think for a moment, and that rattles you for the rest of your life.

Oh, fuck . . .
My little Proustian madeleine . . .
Fine, I didn't think about all that at the time, of course. Besides, I didn't think about it at all since it was tattooed into my skin.
Plus I didn't have time to think because I was making a big arc behind my back with my Francky's walking stick, which was as beautiful as a piece of Van Cleef jewelry, and which I smashed to pieces with a direct hit the face of this gentleman with a crewcut who had just raised a hand against a child.
A direct hit.
Face smashed.
Nose gone.
Mouth gone.
Everything.

Only blood, between his fingers and all over his face.

And squeals.
Pig squeals, of course.

Oh what a mess . . .
Plus, because of my brusque gesture and my raised stick, the donkey got scared and took off at a triple gallop for Kathmandu with all our provisions on his back.
Oh what a mess . . .

And since everyone looked at me as though I'd done him in, I started in again in order to resuscitate the bastard who had dared to hit a sweet little boy:
"So?" I said in my unrecognizable voice that I used for fomenting rebellion. "Do you feel that? Do you see what happens when someone is hit by surprise? Do you see how unpleasant it is? Never do that again, got it? Because next time I'll kill you."
And as he wasn't able to answer me since he was sucking on his cracked teeth, I continued:
"Don't worry, I'm going to get out of here pronto because I can't stand your dirty fascist mouth anymore, but I'm going to tell you one last thing before I leave, asshole . . . Hey, look at me . . . You hear me? Well then listen good: you see, pal, there . . . (and at the same time I was saying that, I didn't dare look in the direction of Francky, of course), (I can't be brave about everything on the same day), well, he's queer . . . and I'm a lesbo . . . oh yeah . . . and that fact, just think, every night, in our little tent, well, it doesn't stop us from doing really filthy things with our bodies, the two of us . . . things you can't even imagine . . . He rarely ejaculates on me, I assure you, but what if a drinking spree goes haywire one evening . . . what if . . . well, if there was a kid born from all that filth between a queer and a lesbian, you know what? Not only would we keep him just to piss you off, but also, we would never hit him. Never,

you understand? We wouldn't ever hurt him the least little bit. Never, never, never . . . And if he really bugged us too much and it prevented us from getting back to our orgy, you know what? We'd bump him off, but we'd do it nicely . . . I swear on the head of your children that he wouldn't suffer. Cross my heart and hope to die. All right now . . . goodbye . . . and fuck off!"

And then I spit at his feet and headed in the direction of my shepherd.

Because I was on the path of Faith, Life, Light, and Truth.

I walked straight ahead for hours and hours.
Straight toward Jesus's mountain.
I didn't even turn around once to see if Francky was following me.

I knew he was following me.

I knew he hated me but was following me anyway.

I knew he hated me but was thanking me at the same time.

And I knew it was really messing up his head.

Because between that fascist ball breaker and his father, there must not have been that much difference . . . The fact is, they belonged to the same cell of the Defenders of Western Christianity . . .

At one point, I froze before some sort of a rift in the mountains.

First, because it was the end of the trail; second, because I hadn't heard any noise behind me for a really long time.

None.

I froze in place and waited.

Blind faith, okay, but I wasn't blind.

Plus, as that poet would say, there is no love.

There are only proofs of love.

I froze in place and looked at my watch.

If he's not here in twenty minutes, I said to myself, I'm giving up the lease on the apartment in the rue de la Fidelité.

No matter how smug I was from time to time, I was still a fragile little thing.

Shit. It was as much for him as for myself that I had blown a fuse.

Liar.

Okay, I admit it. It was only for myself.

Not even for myself . . . But for a little girl I knew when I was little . . .

A little girl whom I never had the chance to tell that even if she smelled during the winter months, she was still my friend and could always join my group of friends and sit next to me in class.

Always.

And forever.

So, okay, there you have it. That's the story.

She got it, her proof of love . . .

If in nineteen minutes, he's not there, I repeated to myself, gritting my teeth, I'll give up the lease on the apartment in the rue de la Fidelité.

And exactly seventeen minutes later, a voice behind my back spit out its venom:

"Hey? You know what? You're a pain in the ass, Morel . . . You're a real pain in the ass!"

I must have cried with happiness.

It was the most beautiful and most romantic declaration of love that anyone had ever made to me in my life.

I turned around, flew into his arms, and—I don't know how I did it— somehow managed to pull both of us into the rift.

We barreled down a rocky slope and ended up all the way at the bottom, smack in the middle of some incredibly thorny bushes and in more or less a thousand pieces.

We crawled as best we could toward an area that was a bit flatter and then gave each other the silent treatment.

Okay, little star, there you have it . . . It's over . . . And if you want to see us again and with bonus features, go back to season 1, episode 1, because I no longer have anything to add.

Hee hee hee.
  I was dreaming that Franck was tickling me.
  Hee hee hee. But . . . uh . . . *stop* that . . .
And when I opened my eyes, I realized I had finally fallen
asleep and those little coochy coos weren't Franck in a dream,
but Donkster robbing my pockets.

"Your new friend wants an apple, it seems . . . "
I straightened up, grimacing, still because of my mangled
arm, and I saw that Franck was there, all calm, sitting on a rock
making coffee.

"Coffee's ready," he said.
"Francky? Is it you? You're not dead?"
"No, not yet . . . Your little stunt didn't work, not so far at
least."
"You haven't broken anything?"
"Yeah, my ankle, I think . . . "
"But uh . . . I'm having a tough time sorting this out . . . you
weren't in a coma?"
"No."
"So what were you doing, then?"
"Sleeping."
Holy fuck, what nerve . . . and all that worry he caused me?

Holy fuck, what nerve . . .

Holy fuck, what nerve!

The man was sleeping . . .

The man was resting . . .

The man was snoozing out in the open . . .

He was simply asleep in the arms of that little slut Morpheus while I gorged on my misery . . .

He sucks.

He let me down.

All that anguish when he had just pretended to pass out . . . All that effort the whole night to make us look good . . . All that work to make our shit look pretty . . . And I had to do it all on the sly because I prefer to inspire respect instead of pity.

Yes, all that digging into my lovely childhood memories to get what would be helpful and to avoid what would serve no purpose other than to drag me even deeper into despair.

All that work to make a silk purse out of a sow's ear . . .

All that bravery . . .

All that tenderness . . .

All that love . . .

And since I was cold . . . And felt alone . . . And was sad . . . And since I had worked so hard to get a dead star to love us . . . and . . . with his handjob fantasy in addition to everything else . . .

Fuck, I was really pissed off then.

Really, really pissed.

"And the donkey? How'd he get here?" I asked.

"I don't know. He was here when I woke up . . . "

"But what path did he take?"

"That path there . . . "

"But . . . uh . . . how did he find us?"

"Don't ask me . . . Yet another jackass stupid enough to care a bit about you . . . "

" . . . "

"Are you mad?"

"Well, yeah, I'm mad, you idiot! I was really worried! And I didn't get a wink of sleep."

"I see that."

Oh I was mad all right, and as for his coffee, he knew where he could shove it.

"You're really angry at me?" he asked with his treacherous little mouth.

" . . . "

"That much?"

" . . . "

"Really that much?"

" . . . "

"Really, really?"

" . . . "

"You were really worried about me?"

" . . . "

"You really thought I was in a coma?"

" . . . "

"You were sad?"

" . . . "

"Really, really sad?"

" . . . "

Yeah, that's it. Keep going, you big idiot. Keep making me feel even more fucking stupid.

Silence.

He hobbled over and placed a steaming cup of coffee next to me with a slice of gingerbread.

I didn't budge.

He sat down as much as he was able with his stiff leg and said to me in a very sweet voice:

"Look at me."

Fuck you.

"Look at me, Billie Jean."

Fine, click . . . click, I cranked my neck three millimeters upward.

"You know, I adore you," he murmured, looking me straight in the eyes. "I adore you more than anyone . . . You know that after all this time, right?"

" . . . "

"Yes, you know. I know you can't help it . . . but for almost four nights in a row you've kept me from sleeping and . . . you're exhausting, you know? Really, really, exhausting . . . So exhausting that sometimes, to deal with you, well, I have to pretend to die . . . You understand that, don't you?"

" . . . "

"Go on, drink your coffee, girl."

I was crying.

So he crawled over to me that morning and, sailor's warning, gave me a hug.

"I th-th-thought you were deaaaaad," I coughed.

"No . . . "

"I th-th-thought you were deaaaaad and that I was g-g-going to kill myself toooooo . . . "

"Oh Billie, you're wearing me out . . . " he sighed. "Go on, drink your coffee and eat a little bit. We still haven't gotten out of this mess."

And I chewed my completely disgusting gingerbread with a marmalade of tears.

And I cried again because I d-d-etested g-g-ginger-b-b-bread.

We took off as best we could, hobbling along in the sun and wind, like in that Yves Montand song.

I had made a splint for Franck with some pieces of wood and some string and he used Donkster like a walker.

We were no longer the ones who guided the providential little donkey; rather it was he who was bringing us back to the fold.

At least that's what we were hoping . . .

To the fold or anywhere.

Anywhere but near my last victim, right?

Right, Donkster? Don't do that to me, okay?

Please.

No, no, he answered, I'm bringing you back to the stable.

I've also had it up to my snout with all of your bullshit . . .

Fine.

We trusted him.

Hobbling along,
in the sun and the
wiiiiiiiiiiiiiind so strong . . .

(Okay, for sure, it sounds better if you have the tune in your head.)

He was really too cute that little donkey.

Well, I'll come back and make off with him one day.

I stopped talking.

Completely.

End of discussion.

Too much emotion, too much exhaustion, too much pain and too much offense taken as well, I have to say.

Franck tried two or three times to start a new topic of conversation, but each time I let it peter out.

Okay, I'm no saint either . . .

He could have spoken to me at least once that night . . .

Just once.

I was as mad as hell at him.

Plus, I had made a fool of myself in front of all those cold stars that couldn't give a damn about my stories.

And I cried and everything.

What a jerk.

Silence.

A big fat silence in the sun and Siberian cold.

And then . . . after about an hour perhaps . . . I finally cracked.

I'd had enough of being all alone with my thoughts since the evening before. Enough, enough. I was really bad company for myself. Plus, I missed him. I missed my bastard of a friend.

So I said:

"Say, it's warm, isn't it?"

And he smiled at me.

Then we talked about this and that like in the good ol' days, but without making the slightest reference to my latest feat. Well, that did it. It was forgotten . . . But there would be others.

After a few minutes, he asked me:

"Why were you laughing?"

"Excuse me?"

"I understood that you were very unhappy and extremely preoccupied with my being in an advanced coma, but at one point, during the night, I heard you laugh. Burst out laughing. Why? Were you thinking about everything you would be able to steal from me in the rue de la Fidelité?"

"No," I smiled. "No . . . It was because I was thinking again about the face of the guys in our class when we finished acting out our scene."

"What scene?"

"Uh, you know . . . the scene from Musset . . . "

"Ah really? I was dying right in front of you at that time and you were thinking about the morons from our class ages ago?"

"Well, yeah . . . "

"And what was the connection?"

"I don't know . . . it just came to me."

"Really?"

"Yes."

"You're really a funny girl, you know?"

" . . . "

Silence.

"Say, you don't mean that play where Perdican marries Rosette in the end?"

And it started up again. We were at it once more.

It was the most timeworn of all our running gags, but fine . . . we would get right to it if that's what he really wanted, and we were off.

"No. He would never have married her."

"Yes, he would have."

"No."

"Absolutely."

"Absolutely not. Guys like that, they don't marry crappy little goose-girls. I know you want to believe it because you're a big romantic from the time of the troubadours, but you're kidding yourself. I come from the same social class as Rosette and I can tell you that at the last minute, he would have taken off . . . He would have had business in Paris or some such excuse . . . Plus his father would never have allowed it. There were still 6,000 écus at stake, I'll remind you."

"He'd have done it."

"No."

"Yes. He'd have married her."

"For what reason?"

"As a nice gesture."

"A nice gesture, my ass. He would have jumped her bones and left her flat with her bastard child, her chickens, and her turkeys.

"You're such a cynic . . . "

"Yes . . . "

"Why?"

"Because I know life better than you do."

"Oh, spare me . . . Stop . . . You're not going to start that again . . .

"I'll stop."

Silence.

"Billie?"

"Yes."

"Do you want to marry me?"

"Excuse me?"

Even the donkey stopped in his tracks.

"Do you want us to get married?"

Uh, never mind, he was just taking a crap . . .

"Why are you talking bullshit?"

"I'm not joking. I've never been more serious in my life."

"But . . . uh . . . "

"Uh, what?"

"Well, we're not exactly on the same team, you know . . . "

"What are you referring to?"

"Well, you know . . . "

"Tell me. Who was the girl who explained to me once that true love has nothing to do with the anatomical chart?"

"I don't know. A little pain in the ass who always wanted to have the last word, I guess."

"Billie . . . "

"Yes?"

"Let's get married . . . The whole world keeps pestering us with their marriage for all, their protests against marriage for all, their counter-protests for all, their hate for all, their prejudices for all, their good feelings for all . . . So why not us? Why not us?"

The idiot was really serious . . .

"And why would we do what other people do?"

"Because one night, I don't know if you remember . . . it was a really long time ago . . . One night, you made me promise never to abandon you because you would only do stupid things without me . . . And I tried, you know . . . I really tried to honor my promise . . . But I wasn't strong enough to succeed. If I was just four steps behind you, you would go crazy again . . . So I would like to marry you so that you'll have fewer little problems in the future . . . We wouldn't tell anyone and it wouldn't changed anything about how we live today, but we would know. We would be aware that this connection exists between us, and we would know it forever."

He was speaking as if I remembered that night . . .

So, he didn't just sleep either . . .

"You know very well that I'll always do stupid things . . . "

"No, that's just it. I'm hoping that it will calm you down a bit."

"What will?"

"Finally having a little bit of family all to yourself."

Silence.

"Say yes, Billie . . . Look, I can't get down on one knee because I'm in too much pain but imagine me doing it . . . Imagine the scene . . . With your little donkey as witness . . . I've been paddling along with you for ten years now and today, I really want to reach the shore . . . "

"For starters, why do you want to marry *me*?"

"Because you're the most beautiful human being I've ever met and will ever meet and I would like it to be you whom I call first if something happens to me too."

"Oh really? Really, well yeah, so . . . " I sighed. "If we're just talking about picking up the phone, count me in . . . Happy to oblige."

Say, little star, your fellow stars look like they're in party mode, but hey . . . go easy with those pills, my little sweetie, because you're really flying high there . . .

Silence.

Silence in the sun and beneath the blue sky.

"So? Why is she smiling stupidly like that, the little Billie?" He said mockingly. "Is she thinking about her wedding night?"

But . . . ooooh . . . uh . . . I wasn't smilingly stupidly at all. On the contrary, I was smiling quite gracefully.

I was smiling because I wasn't wrong.
Uh no . . .

I was really pleased with myself because I was right again: A good story, especially a love story, always ends with marriage, and singing, dancing, a tambourine, and so on.
Ah yes . . .

La, la, li li . . . la la . . .

Dearest Henri Bertaud du Chazaud—many thanks.

ABOUT THE AUTHOR

Born in Paris in 1970, Anna Gavalda's first published work was the critically acclaimed collection of short stories *I Wish Someone Were Waiting for Me Somewhere*, which sold over half a million copies in her native France and was published in the US by Riverhead in 2003. She is also the author of *Someone I Loved* and the international bestseller *Hunting and Gathering* (Riverhead, 2007), which was made into a film starring Audrey Tatou and Daniel Auteil. Gavalda lives in Paris.